# *Embracing Forever*

Sheryl Lister

This is a work of fiction. Names, characters, places, and incidents are either products of the writer's imagination or are used fictitiously and are not to be construed as real. Any resemblance to actual events, locales, organizations, or persons, living or dead, is entirely coincidental.

Embracing Forever

Book ISBN: 978-1976566998



NYLA Publishing
350 7th Avenue, Suite 2003, NY 10001, New York.
http://www.nyliterary.com

## Acknowledgements

My Heavenly Father, thank You for Your sufficient grace.

To my husband, Lance: your love, support and encouragement is what keeps me going.

Brandi, Maia, Riana, Otis, Sr., Otis Jr. and Jace, Mom (Grandma) loves you!

Thank you to my friends and family for your consistent support.

Leslie (Elle), Sherelle and Angie, I love you ladies!

A huge thank you to David Ruggles at Fuqua Physical Therapy for all those make-your-back-better massages and for making me laugh through the pain.

To all of my readers: thank you from the bottom of my heart.

Latoya Smith, your editorial guidance is priceless. Thank you.

A very special thank you to my agent, Sarah E. Younger and Natanya Wheeler. I appreciate you more than I can say. You ladies are miracle workers!

# The Pact

Raven Holloway followed her three best friends across the grounds of the Rosewood Estates and dropped down into one of the four cushioned wicker chairs set up around a table. She toed off her heels and groaned. "I don't know how women wear these things every day. My feet are killing me." Though she didn't mind dressing up occasionally, Raven was far more comfortable in jeans, sweats, a tee and sneakers.

"Look at them. They're so happy."

She shook her head. Quinn Jacobs tended to be the hopeless romantic of the group. Raven glanced over her shoulder at the newlyweds. "Yes, they do, and I think Owen will be good for Ava." Raven, Quinn, Mackenzie Cannon and Ryleigh Fields—best friends since childhood—had all come back to their small hometown of Rosewood Heights, South Carolina to serve as bridesmaids for their friend, Ava Prescott. While each of them had moved away to pursue their careers, Ava had been the only one to stay.

A waiter approached to take their drink order. Dinner wouldn't be served for another hour, but the bar was free and flowing.

"I'll have a mojito," Mackenzie said.

Raven stared. "Isn't that like your third or fourth one?"

"Sixth, but who's counting? And this *is* a celebration."

She chuckled. "Can't argue with that. I'll take one, too," Raven told the waiter.

"I'll have a margarita," Ryleigh chimed in.

Quinn put up a finger. "Make that two."

They continued to laugh, catch up and talk about how it felt to be back home. They all lived in different states, but made a practice of having a conference call at least once a month. Raven admittedly missed the slower pace and all the greenery, but loved her job as a physical therapist in Los Angeles.

The waiter returned and placed their glasses on the table in front of them. The women thanked him and he departed with a nod.

Quinn picked up her glass and took a sip. "I think we should toast." Once they all had their glasses, she lifted hers high. "Here's to us all finding that special one and saying 'I do' by this time next year."

"Oh, hell no." Ryleigh placed her glass down with a thud.

Mackenzie shook her head. "The only thing I'm saying 'I do' to is one night with that tall, mouth-watering best man standing over there." She gestured in his direction.

Raven just stared. It took a moment for her to finally find her voice. "Are you *crazy*?"

"No," Quinn said. "We're thirty years old. I don't want to be pushing a stroller when I'm fifty."

Raven couldn't see herself pushing a stroller at all.

Quinn scooted forward in her chair. "Think about it. Just about everybody we know has gotten married in the last three years, yet we're all still single. Wouldn't it be nice to have a warm, hard body to snuggle up to every night? To not have to worry about those awkward bar or club meetings? I mean how hard could it be?" She lifted her glass again. "Come on," she pleaded. "We can do this. Let's make this a best friend challenge."

Quinn turned that sad look on them and Raven groaned. She slowly reached for her glass. "I can't believe I'm about to do this," she mumbled.

Mackenzie and Ryleigh muttered a curse, but followed suit.

Quinn smiled. "To finding that special one and saying 'I do' by this time next year."

They reluctantly touched glasses and sipped.

Raven took a big gulp of her mojito. She needed it. *What the hell did I just agree to?*

Immediately after the toast, Ryleigh slammed her glass onto the table and stormed off, no doubt heading to the bar.

"I'll see you guys later," Mac said.

Raven smiled and shook her head when she saw Mac walk over to the best man.

Quinn tossed back the rest of some drink that had been sitting on the table. "I'll be back." She mumbled something about the best one winning, stuck her feet back into her shoes and strutted off.

Alone now, she leaned her head back against the cushion, closed her eyes and tried to process what she'd just done. Her track record with men had her batting a big fat zero, so it made no sense to agree to something so stupid, pact or not. She opened her eyes, lifted her glass to her lips and froze, her gaze connecting with reason number one why men and marriage were off her list. Shawn Lewis. Her first boyfriend. They'd started dating in their junior year and both had planned to attend college together at the University of South Carolina, get degrees in physical therapy then come back and open up a rehabilitation clinic in Rosewood Heights. That dream died the moment she caught him kissing another girl at the homecoming dance during their senior year.

When the October early application period came around a month later, she researched colleges that were furthest from home and settled on California State University, Long Beach. One, it was clear across the country and two, her mother's sister and family lived in Los Angeles, so she would have some family nearby. Her mother hadn't been too happy, but Raven excelled and opted to stay in California once she finished school. Much to her mother's disappointment, Simeon, Raven's younger brother, fell in love with the area after one visit and followed Raven out to the West Coast. He had graduated from Stanford Law School just over two years ago.

Shawn smiled. Raven didn't. Last she heard, he was on his third or fourth marriage. She shifted her attention and took a sip of her drink. After Shawn, there had been the guy in college who, after two dates, thought she "owed" him for all the money he'd spent feeding her. After refusing to sleep with him, Raven had slapped a twenty-dollar bill in his palm and told him to keep the change. Her bad luck didn't stop there. She'd had to endure guys who cheated, got angry when she wouldn't give them the "hookup" with the professional athletes that frequented the rehab clinic where she worked, or who were so jealous of her three male friends, they tried to give her an ultimatum. A smile curved her lips as she thought about Bryson, Jerome and Kendrick. With them she didn't have to worry about the drama that plagued her with dating. And she liked her life that way.

Raven searched the grounds for Quinn, Mac and Ryleigh and sighed when she didn't see them. She couldn't do this. They'd been doing these crazy challenges as long as Raven could remember and for the first time, she contemplated telling them she changed her mind. On second thought, they didn't need to know.

# Chapter One

*Eight months later*

"Ow!"

Raven shook her head and continued the therapeutic massage. "Chris, for sixteen weeks a year, not including playoffs, you're smashed by three-hundred pound linebackers. Surely you can handle this little bitty massage. Chris Powell was a tight end for the local professional football team. He had suffered a back injury at the end of the season and after undergoing surgery a couple of months ago, had been sent to the state of the art rehabilitation center where she worked as a physical therapist.

"Yeah, but when a beautiful woman is giving me a massage, pain is not something that I want to feel."

"Well, this isn't the wine and candles kind of massage. It's a make-your-back-better-so-you-can-get-back-on-the-field massage." She finished up, attached electrodes for the electrical stimulation and turned on the machine. The machine worked by sending stimulating pulses across the skin and along the nerve endings to help with pain management. "How's that?" she asked as she adjusted the strength.

"That's good. Thanks."

Raven covered his back with a towel and placed a bag of ice on top. She set the timer for fifteen minutes, turned off the lights and exited the room, pulling the door partially closed. She washed her hands and went to chart Chris's progress. Her phone buzzed in her pocket. She pulled it out and read the text from Darren Hayes, her boyfriend of the past four months, confirming their date for the evening. He'd said he had something to discuss with her and she wondered what could be so important that it warranted going out on a Thursday night. Fridays were her early days with a start time of seven and she dearly hoped Darren didn't plan on making it a long evening.

Raven saw her final two clients and rushed home, or what passed for rushing as she made her way through the LA traffic. By the time she arrived, she barely had time to shower and dress. She slipped into a sleeveless eggplant-colored sheath silhouette dress and black strappy sandals then ran a brush through her straight shoulder-length strands and added a coat of bronze lipstick. Satisfied with her look, she dropped the lipstick back into the cosmetic bag just as the doorbell rang.

She turned off the lights, picked up her purse and wrap and walked down the hallway of her condo to open the front door. "Hey, Darren," she said, stepping back so he could enter.

Darren's eyes widened. "Wow! You look beautiful." He lowered his head and kissed her.

"Thanks. You don't look so bad yourself," Raven said with a smile. With his tall, slender build in the tailored gray suit and dark good looks, he didn't look bad at all.

He slid an arm around her waist. "You think so?" He kissed her once more. "Mmm, I'm looking forward to sharing these kisses every day."

She gave him a questioning look.

He merely smiled and gestured toward the door. "Shall we?"

She locked the door and let him escort her out to his late model Lexus. Though the sun had begun to set, the late May temperatures still hovered in the upper seventies. At this rate, the summer promised to be a hot one.

As they settled into the car and pulled out onto the road,

Darren asked, "How was your day?"

"Pretty busy. I had back-to-back clients all day. And yours?"

He smiled and turned her way briefly. "*Very* good." He worked as a supervisor at a press release distribution company.

Raven waited for him to say more, but he just refocused on the road and said nothing. They made small talk for a few minutes, then she asked, "So what's this important news you wanted to talk about?"

"I'm saving it for while we're having dinner."

She shifted in her seat to stare at him. What did he have up his sleeve and why did she have a weird feeling in the pit of her stomach? Minutes later, he pulled up to the Beverly Wilshire Hotel and turned the car over to the valet. Inside, he escorted her to CUT by Wolfgang Puck and she offered up a silent thank you that she'd opted for a nice dress instead of the slacks she had originally selected. Despite it being a Thursday evening, the restaurant was fairly crowded. Evidently Darren had made reservations because it only took a moment for them to be seated.

"Comfortable?" Darren asked as she slid into the booth.

"Yes. Thank you. This is very nice." They'd gone to a couple of nice restaurants before, but nothing like this.

"I thought we'd do it up big tonight." He winked and lowered his head to the menu.

*What is this man up to?* Raven surveyed him a moment longer, then opened her own menu. There were so many choices of steaks—prime from Nebraska and Illinois, Wagyu from Idaho and Japan—and some at prices that widened her eyes. She didn't know where to begin. She glanced up when the server came to take their drink order and couldn't mask her surprise when Darren ordered an expensive bottle of wine. She waited until the young woman departed before speaking. "Are we celebrating?"

Darren smiled. "As a matter of fact, we are. And as soon as the wine arrives, I'll tell you why."

All kinds of alarms went off in her head. It didn't take long for the server to return with the wine and fill their glasses. Raven thanked her and smoothed her napkin in her lap.

"I have some exciting news." He leaned forward. "I've been promoted to regional marketing manager."

She smiled. "Congratulations. That's definitely worth celebrating." She lifted her glass. "To your continued success."

Darren touched his glass against hers and held her gaze as they sipped. He set his glass down and grasped Raven's hand. "There's something else I'm hoping to celebrate. I know we've only been dating four months, but I'm ready to take things to the next level."

*Next level?* Okay, Raven liked Darren well enough and, although she only had four months left on that stupid marriage pact she'd made with her friends, she didn't yet feel all the warm and fuzzy stuff that went along with falling in love. "What do you mean?"

"I—"

"Raven? Is that you?"

She whipped her head around and saw Chris standing there with his former teammate, Bernard Harris, who had retired a couple of years ago after a career-ending injury, and who had also been one of her clients at the rehab center. "Yep, it's me. It's good to see you, Bernard. Retirement looks good on you."

"Thanks. I'm enjoying it." He bent and gave her a quick hug.

Chris grinned. "Girl, you clean up pretty well."

Raven smiled and shook her head. She made introductions. The three men shook hands, but Darren didn't appear to be pleased by the interruption.

"Darren, you lucked out. Raven has the best hands in the business." Chris shot her a teasing wink.

Darren's jaw tightened.

She rolled her eyes. "I think you're over exaggerating, Chris. Shouldn't you be at home resting your back or doing your stretches?"

Bernard chuckled. "Come on, Chris. Leave Raven alone." He turned to Darren. "Nice meeting you, man and sorry for the interruption." He placed a hand on Raven's shoulder. "Good seeing you, Raven."

She reached up and squeezed his hand. "You too. Take care of yourself."

"I'll see you next Tuesday," Chris said. "You two enjoy your dinner."

Raven followed their departure with a smile. There was never a dull moment with Chris around. He kept the rehab center lively with his humor. "Sorry. What were you saying?"

"Are you always so *cozy* with your clients?" Darren asked tightly.

Raven lifted an eyebrow. "Exactly what are you insinuating? I act the same way with every one of my clients, regardless of who they are."

"Have you given any more thought to the offer I mentioned?"

"No." He had expressed his dislike of her working with all the young men and had suggested she change jobs so *he* wouldn't have to worry about some client flirting with her. At the time, she hadn't put much stock into it, thinking he'd been kidding, but now she realized he'd been quite serious.

He took a sip of his wine. "My friend won't be able to hold the position forever."

"He doesn't need to hold it at all. I like my job and I have no intention of changing it."

He shook his head. "You know, I thought we might be moving toward something more permanent, but if you're not willing to compromise…"

Raven couldn't believe her ears. "*Compromise?* So, because *you're* insecure about me working with a bunch of athletes, I'm supposed to do what? Take a position in some nursing home so you can be comfortable?" She didn't realize she had raised her voice until the couple in the next booth turned around. She took a deep breath. "You're right about one thing…we are moving toward something permanent." She tossed her napkin on the table. "Take me home." She slid out of the booth and stalked to the front. Obviously, this relationship was not going to work if he couldn't respect her or her career choice.

Darren joined her a moment later. "Thank you for embarrassing me in front of a room full of people," he whispered harshly.

She laughed him off. "You're kidding right?"

"Do I look like I'm kidding?" He latched on to her arm and jerked her to him. "It wasn't enough that you raised your voice to me, but you basically flirted with two men right in front of my face."

Raven snatched her arm away. "Take your hand off me. I embarrassed *you*? I wasn't the one acting like a spoiled child in front of my clients."

Darren glared at her. "We wouldn't have a problem if you would just be reasonable and meet me halfway."

"So that's what you're calling it. Reasonable." Raven shook her head at his audacity. Not only had he disrespected her, but he had also put his hands on her. If he felt bold enough to do something like this to her in public, there was no telling how far he'd go in private. She had no intentions of signing on for any type of abuse. "We're done. *Permanently.*" She left him standing there, went back inside and marched toward the restroom. He had some nerve grabbing her. She unconsciously rubbed the spot on her arm. Raven took a deep breath to regain her composure, pulled out her phone and called a cab. She ventured back outside moments later and took a discreet look around. Darren was nowhere to be seen. The fact that he'd left solidified in her mind that they would have never worked. Ten minutes later, the cab drove up. She collapsed onto the seat, closed her eyes and let all of her emotions rise to the surface. She didn't know why she bothered. Marriage pact or not, she was done.

* * *

Bryson Montgomery sat in his office at Impressions Community Center Saturday morning making a grocery list for next weekend's camping trip. This would be their second trip and he scheduled it the first weekend in June again, right after the school year ended. The time frame seemed to work well for everyone. He had opened the youth center two years ago after leaving his job as an inpatient clinical psychologist and, although it was hard work, he hadn't regretted it for one moment.

His friend and business partner, Jerome Smith, poked his head in the door. "Hey, Bryson. The new camping supplies were just delivered. I'll start opening boxes and making sure everything is there."

Bryson nodded. "I'll be there as soon as I finish making this grocery list and emailing the tech company who agreed to donate new laptops." They wouldn't be shopping until next Thursday, but he wanted to start early to ensure he didn't miss anything. He pulled out and compared the previous year's list, made some additions and put it aside. Turning toward his computer, he sent a reply to the tech company thanking them for their donation and asking for possible delivery dates. He hoped to have the laptops installed by the time the summer school program started at the end of the month. During the year, the center opened after school only, but during the summer opened ten hours per day. Bryson hit the *send* button, stood and went to help Jerome. There had to be thirty or forty large boxes stacked in the meeting room. "Did we order all this?"

Jerome cut open another box and chuckled. "Yep. I didn't realize we ordered this much, either. The camping trip will be over by the time we finish going through everything."

"Good thing Kendrick said he'd be here to help this morning." Kendrick Johnson, Jerome and Bryson had all met and become friends in college. Kendrick worked as a high school calculus teacher and volunteered his time in the summer tutoring math.

"Is Raven coming, too?"

Bryson smiled at the mention of his best friend's name. "Yeah. She said she'd help." He'd met Raven Holloway when she was a freshman and he a junior in a psychology class when they were both complaining about the classroom desks not being left-handed friendly. Over the past twelve years, she had been there through every high and low in his life and her friendship meant everything to him.

"Good. Then we may be done before the bus loads."

He laughed and picked up a box. They'd gotten through a good ten boxes before Kendrick joined them. Raven arrived not long after. Immediately, Bryson noticed she wasn't her normal smart-alecky self.

He pulled her aside. "Hey, everything okay?"

Raven smiled. "Fine. Why?"

Bryson frowned. "I don't know. You seem a little out of sorts."

"Just had a long day yesterday, that's all."

He didn't believe her for a minute. They'd known each other too long and something didn't feel right.

Raven placed a hand on her hip. "Are you going to stare at me all day or get to work?"

He grinned. "The mouth is back."

She bumped him playfully and pointed toward a box. "Work, Bryson. I don't want to be here all day."

"Me, either." They planned to go out afterwards, something the four friends did at least once a month. It took three hours to finish inventorying the boxes and putting the supplies away.

"Man, how much stuff did you two order?" Kendrick asked. "I thought we'd never finish."

Bryson held up his hands in mock surrender. "Hey, Rome did all the ordering on this one."

"We have more kids going this year and some of the

donated stuff was old and worn, so it had to be replaced. We can't have the kids sleeping in tents with little tears and sleeping bags so thin you can see through them," Jerome added.

Raven laughed. "Well, I'm all for that. Just because I have to sleep on the ground doesn't mean I want to feel it." She glanced down at her watch. "It's after three. Are we going to eat or what?"

"Yeah, we are," Kendrick said. "Bryse and Rome will keep us here all night."

Bryson shook his head. "Shut up, Ken. Like you didn't hold us up many a night working on some crazy calculus problem."

"What? I know you're not—"

"Yeah, yeah." Raven pushed Kendrick toward the door. "You guys can talk trash while we eat."

They all laughed and filed out. Bryson locked up the center and they stood in the parking lot for a few minutes deciding where to eat, agreeing on a nearby bar and grill.

Once there, they had a twenty-minute wait before being led to a table.

Jerome picked up his menu. "I'm so hungry I could eat two horses. I'll order a couple of appetizers to hold us until the meal."

By the time the hostess came to take the drink order, they were ready to give their food order, as well. Bryson saw Raven check her phone, then frown. Something was going on with her. He caught her attention and mouthed, "You okay?"

Raven nodded, looked away and turned her attention to whatever Jerome and Kendrick were saying.

Throughout the meal, he contributed to the conversation, but kept one eye on her. More than once, he noticed her go quiet and a look of sadness cross her face. However, each time, it disappeared and she appeared to be her old self again.

Afterwards, they parted ways in the parking lot. Bryson walked Raven to her car. "So, are you going to tell me what's going on with you? And don't try to tell me it's nothing. I've known you a long time."

"Just some stuff I need to work through. Nothing for you to worry about."

He studied her a long moment. "You sure?"

She smiled. "Positive. Thanks, though."

He hugged her and kissed her cheek. "If you change your mind and want to talk, you know where to find me."

"I will. Goodnight."

"Night, Raven. Drive safe and text me when you get home."

Raven chuckled. "Yes, *Dad*. You've been saying the same thing for the past twelve years."

"Yep. And I'll be saying it for the next twelve and beyond." He held her door open while she got in and closed it behind her. Bryson waited until she drove off before going to his car. He didn't believe for one second that everything was okay. But he planned to get to the bottom of it, sooner rather than later.

# Chapter Two

Friday, a week later, Raven continued to be plagued with thoughts of her breakup. She didn't know what incensed her more, the fact that Darren had asked her to change her job or his belief that she would defer to him like they were somewhere in the nineteenth century. And as much as she tried to deny it, adding another failed relationship to the already lengthy list had devastated her. Pushing her feelings aside, she concentrated on helping two mothers load boxes of food onto the bus for the camping trip. She had taken the day off and hoped being away for the weekend would help restore her balance.

She turned at the sound of male laughter. Bryson, Kendrick and Jerome always seemed to have more fun than the kids. All three stood over six feet, had well-defined muscular builds and gave new definition to good-looking. Whereas Jerome and Kendrick wore their hair cut short, Bryson sported shoulder-length locs. She knew more than a few single mothers braved the bugs and dirt just to get close to them. However, their efforts continued to go unnoticed. Too bad she couldn't say the same thing. Bryson had either texted or called her every day over the past several days to check on her. As he'd told her, he knew her well.

"I don't know what I was thinking volunteering to sleep on the ground for the next two nights," one mother said sliding the last box in the storage compartment. "This child better be glad I love him."

Raven burst out laughing. "I'm going to see if the guys need anything else." She was still chuckling when she approached them.

"Ms. Holloway, is it time to leave *yet*?" a student asked as she passed him.

"Just a few more minutes, Casey." Bryson wanted to be on the road no later than two o'clock to ensure they arrived with a few hours of daylight left, a half an hour from now.

"O-*kay*." The ten-year old shuffled off.

Raven shook her head. Whereas the parent's enthusiasm level hovered somewhere around zero, the kids were bouncing off the walls with excitement. "Hey, Bryse. Is there anything else that needs to be loaded?"

Bryson shifted his gaze from the list in his hand to Raven. "Nope. I think we have everything. I just need to grab the first aid kit from my office and we'll be ready. You can start loading the bus." He paused. "Those things get straightened out?"

"They're fine. I'll see you in a minute." His penetrating stare told her he didn't believe a word she said. She left before he could say anything else.

Thirty minutes later, they were on the road. The lively chatter on the bus made Raven temporarily forget about her problems. She laughed at the corny jokes told by the kids and adults and shook her head at Jerome when he challenged a couple of teenagers to a dance-off that would be held around the campfire during the weekend.

The adults were slow to emerge from the bus when they arrived at Big Bear Lake more than two hours later. However, the kids bounded off with enough energy to power a small city. The first order of business was unloading all the supplies and pitching tents. Bryson and Kendrick had driven their trucks, which contained several large coolers filled with ice to store the refrigerated foods, as well as camping stoves and grills. Raven was in charge of assigning tents and setting up the cooking and cleaning schedule. The thirty students would take shifts, along with some adult supervision.

This year Bryson had been able to secure a campsite close to the bathrooms and lake, and Raven looked forward to sitting by the water after lights out. By the time everything had been set up and dinner served, it was almost seven and the kids dove into the barbeque chicken, corn on the cob and baked beans as if they hadn't eaten in days. She had to admit the guys had really outdone themselves with the meal.

"All right everybody," Bryson's voice rang out. "Once we're done with the cleanup, we'll meet around the campfire to talk about the schedule for the weekend. It'll be lights out early tonight since we have a long day tomorrow."

Raven pitched in to help with the cleanup and it took less than half an hour for them to wash the dishes and pick up the trash. By nine, the last traces of light had dissipated, leaving a black, cloudless sky studded with stars. She walked the short distance to the lake and took a seat on one of the metal benches. She inhaled the sweet night air and exhaled slowly. The area reminded her of home. Growing up, Raven could always be found near one of the lakes. The water seemed to give her a sense of peace and she did her best thinking during those times. Tonight, however, that peace was nowhere to be found.

For some reason, every guy she had dated over the past decade either wanted to change her or felt threatened by her friendship with Bryson, Jerome and Kendrick. And this latest episode with Darren, from him grabbing her to basically giving her an ultimatum—her job or him—strengthened her belief that love just wasn't for her. Raven felt the sting of hot tears burning her eyes and forced them back. She hated crying and did her best to avoid it at all costs. She heard a rustling behind her and turned to see Jerome approaching. She quickly brought her emotions under control and hoped the darkness covered her distress.

"Raven." Jerome took a seat on the bench next to her. "Girl, you need to let somebody know where you're going. I nearly had a heart attack when I couldn't find you."

Raven laughed softly. "I'm a grown woman, Jerome."

He slanted her a glance. "And that means what? You know Bryse, Ken and I think of you as a little sister and will always be concerned about your wellbeing. You ought to be used to it by now."

She shook her head. "You guys need to get a life."

"We have lives. Pretty good ones, I might add. Now, why are you out here in the dark all alone?"

"Just thinking…relaxing." She felt his gaze on her, but refused to look his way. He was about as bad as Bryson.

"Hmm. Thinking. Anything you want to talk about?"

"Nope. I'm good. Everybody sleep?"

"Just about. I still heard a few whispers from a couple of the tents when I came out, though." Jerome leaned forward, rested his forearms on his thighs and clasped his hands together. He was silent for a long moment then said softly, "If you want to talk about it, we'll be here for you."

"I know." Raven didn't know why she thought they wouldn't be able to figure out something was bothering her. They always knew. Just like she knew when they had anything going on. Lately, it seemed that she was the only one having issues in the relationship department. Pride and embarrassment kept her from confiding in them at the moment. Eventually, she'd tell them, though. She always did.

He placed a brotherly kiss on her cheek and stood. "I'm going to leave you to your silence. Don't stay out here too long."

She smiled. "I won't. Thanks, Jerome." She watched him saunter back the way he came, knowing most likely he'd still keep her in his sights. She couldn't ask for better friends.

Her mind automatically shifted to her best girlfriends and that ridiculous pact. Mackenzie and Ryleigh—the two most adamant about not being in a committed relationship—had gotten married, leaving only Quinn and herself on the countdown clock.

Hopefully, Quinn was having better luck. Sighing deeply, Raven stood and started back to her tent. She'd had enough of this thing called love.

* * *

"Okay, everybody. You have free time for the next three hours." Bryson glanced down at his watch—two-thirty. "Those of you on dinner duty, we'll start around five, so rest up." They had spent much of that Saturday on a scavenger hunt and completing a two-mile hike.

"Thank goodness," one of the mothers said, removing her backpack and dropping down onto one of the benches. "I don't think I'm ever going to have feeling in my legs and feet again."

He chuckled. "You did great, Mrs. Jones. A hot shower and a couple hours of rest, and you'll be good as new."

The kids and parents trudged to their tents, some of them reemerging a few minutes later with chaperones to head over to the showers. Bryson decided to wait until the bathroom was clear before taking his, and instead, grabbed a bottle of water from a cooler, sat and drained the contents in one long gulp.

"Thirsty?" Kendrick chuckled and took a seat on the opposite bench.

"Something like that." He reached into the cooler, got another bottle and handed it to Kendrick.

"Thanks." He opened it and took a long swig. "The younger kids did well. I admit, I was a little concerned, but they hung in there with minimal complaint."

"They did, and you were the perfect person to lead them." They laughed.

Jerome sauntered over and sat on the edge of the bench. "What are you two laughing about?"

"I was telling Ken he was the perfect person to head up the younger kids," Bryson answered.

"Amen. Give me the older ones any day."

Kendrick shook his head. "Both of you should get a little practice, so you'll be ready when you have your own."

Jerome held up his hands. "No, thanks. I'm quite happy with my single status. Just because Sandra has got you all locked up doesn't mean we need to follow suit." He and Bryson did a fist bump.

"I'm telling you, it's great to have that one special woman. I love not having to worry about the crazy dating scene anymore. Y'all should try it. Bryse, aren't you still seeing that woman you met last year?"

"I'm not *seeing* Whitney. We just hooked up for dinner or something whenever she came to town." Bryson had met the human resource recruiter at a business conference a year and a half ago. One thing led to another and they'd ended up in her hotel room. Neither of them was looking for anything permanent and he didn't do long-distance relationships. Whitney living in Seattle definitely qualified.

Jerome clapped him on the shoulder. "It's the *or something* you're more interested in, I bet."

"Not really. Most of the time, we met for drinks or dinner." Aside from the night in her hotel room, they'd slept together only once more, and that had been close to six months ago.

"And the rest of the time…?" Kendrick asked with a grin.

Bryson held up two fingers. "Twice. And I haven't talked to her in probably six months. For all I know she could've found somebody and be planning her wedding."

"Would that bother you?"

"Rome, why would it bother me that a woman I have no designs on finds someone?" Bryson shrugged. "If she did, more power to her." They had a good time together, but she didn't give him anything he couldn't get from another woman. "And, unlike this clown," he gestured to Jerome, "I'm not opposed to marriage. I just haven't found this *special* woman you're referring to. If and when I do, I'll let you know."

"You guys might want to settle down soon. It would be ugly watching you trying to play catch with your kids at fifty while balancing on a cane," Kendrick said with a chuckle.

Jerome opened his mouth to give Kendrick what Bryson knew would be a mouthful and Bryson said warningly, "Remember the kids."

"Wait until we get back, Ken. I'll show you old. I'll still have game way past fifty and I won't be needing a cane," Jerome muttered.

The three men exploded with laughter. Bryson put his finger to his lips, signaling for them to be quiet. "Don't wake everybody up."

Still chuckling, Jerome said, "Right. I need these couple of hours." He glanced around, then leaned forward. "Have you guys talked to Raven?"

Bryson shifted to face Jerome. "No, but something's up with her."

"Yeah, there is. Last night, after everyone went to bed, I found her sitting by the lake. I could swear she was crying before I got there."

Kendrick frowned. "That's not like her. I can count on one hand the number of times she's cried. Once, when she thought she wasn't going to get into grad school and twice because some jerk broke her heart." He paused as if thinking. "Isn't she dating some guy named Darren?"

"Far as I know," Bryson said. "But he'd better not be the reason for her tears." The last man Raven had dated cheated on her and it had taken a great deal of restraints on all their parts to not beat the guy to a pulp. He couldn't stand to see Raven cry and he truly hoped Darren wasn't to blame. He stood and stretched. "I'm going to shower and chill for a while. It'll be time to start dinner before I know it."

"Go relax, Chef Bryse. Jerome and I will keep an eye out."

Shaking his head at Kendrick, Bryson headed to his tent, gathered his toiletries and went to shower. Afterward, he returned to his tent. He stretched out on the inflatable mattress, set the alarm for an hour and closed his eyes.

It seemed as though Bryson had just drifted off the sleep when he heard the soft beeping on his phone. He shut off the alarm, sat up and dragged a hand down his face. Dinner wouldn't start for another thirty minutes, but he wanted to start setting up to ensure the meal prep would go smoothly.

With the help of Raven, three of the parents and the assigned students, Bryson laid out a feast of grilled steaks, mashed potatoes, green beans and rolls. They also had homemade macaroni and cheese, courtesy of one of the mothers who wanted to express her thanks.

Following dinner and cleanup, the group did most of the packing so they would be ready to leave soon after breakfast, then gathered around the fire for s'mores. The campfire also served as the time when students, especially the high schoolers shared their successes from the previous year and goals for the next.

Students shared everything from raising their grades and passing hard classes to avoiding detention and successfully completing anger management sessions. He was proud of all their accomplishments and had high hopes for the upcoming school year. They ended with a dance-off between Jerome and the two students he'd challenged on the bus ride. Bryson thought he would hurt himself laughing at his buddy. While Jerome could keep the rhythm reasonably well, the age gap was readily apparent because after two minutes, Jerome's breathing sounded like someone who'd just run a marathon.

Once everyone had gone to bed, he, Kendrick and Raven teased him mercilessly.

"Kendrick, you might need to help him get to the showers tonight," Raven teased. "He's moving kind of slow."

Jerome scowled. "Ha ha. Good night."

Kendrick placed a hand on Jerome's shoulder. "Come on, old man. I think I have some Bengay for all those aches you're going to have tomorrow."

He shrugged Kendrick's hand off and strode away.

"See you guys in the morning," Kendrick said, chuckling.

Bryson and Raven both called out, "Good night."

On the heels of their departure, one of the mothers approached. Bryson rose to his feet. "You need something, Mrs. Peterson?"

"No. I just wanted to thank you for what you're doing with these kids and my son. Because of you…all of you, Anthony is doing well in school for the first time in years," Mrs. Peterson said emotionally. "He's not angry or talking about ending his life."

"I'm glad we could be there for Anthony and your family." He felt his own emotions rising. He'd taken a huge risk leaving his hospital job, but in his mind, the payoff had been worth it, especially hearing how the center has changed the lives of the students it served.

"Well, I'll let you two get back to your conversation. See you in the morning."

After she left, Bryson sat with his head bowed, reflecting on her words.

Raven rubbed his back. "You okay?"

"Yeah." She knew his history and the driving force behind his decision to start the center. He glanced over to see her still viewing him with concern. "I'm fine, but I know you're not and, once we get home, you and I are going to talk."

She rubbed her hands up and down her thighs and stared out into the dark. "I know."

Bryson slung an arm around her shoulder and kissed her temple. "Whatever it is, we can work it out. You know we're all here for you."

Raven gave him a small smile and leaned against his shoulder. "You guys always have been and I appreciate it more than you know." She patted Bryson's thigh. "If you don't need anything, I'm going to turn in."

"I'm good. See you in the morning."

"Night, Bryse."

He watched until she ducked into her tent then stared up

into the star-studded sky. Raven's melancholy mood had him concerned. He never recalled her being this down because of a breakup and prayed it wasn't something more serious, like an illness. Pushing to his feet, he surveyed the area one last time to make sure everything had been secured before heading to his own tent. As he passed Raven's tent, he saw the light from her lantern and toyed with asking her talk now, but nixed the idea. He wanted their conversation to take place somewhere private, with no interruptions. By this time tomorrow, he vowed to have all the answers.

* * *

While Bryson always enjoyed the camping trip, this time he was chomping at the bit to get home. It took just over two hours to get back to the center and he was glad to see the parents waiting in the parking lot. He and Jerome made certain each student got off safely, and then joined Kendrick and Raven unloading the supplies. They put away all the things that needed to be refrigerated and stacked the other crates and boxes against the wall in the conference room. He and Jerome would take care of them tomorrow. The early afternoon return gave them a chance to recover before having to be back Monday morning.

Jerome came in with the last box. "Well, another successful trip down. You want to go get something to eat first?"

Keeping his voice low, Bryson said, "I need to take a raincheck. I'm going to follow Raven home and see what's up."

"Good. Call me later and let me know how she is."

"Okay."

"I'll lock up. Just go take care of our girl."

They shared a brotherly hug and Bryson went back outside. He found Raven talking to Kendrick. "Thanks for all your help this weekend."

"You're welcome," Kendrick said. "I'll talk to you guys later this week. Are we doing our Friday night dinner?"

Raven nodded. "I don't have anything planned, so I'm in."

"Me, either," Bryson said. "Check to see if Jerome is free. If he is, we can set it up midweek."

"Okay. Let me go ask." Kendrick hugged Raven and kissed her cheek, brought Bryson in for a one-arm hug and waved.

Bryson turned to Raven. "Ready?"

"Yep."

He walked her to her car and held the door open. "I'll be right behind you." She nodded and he closed the door, got into his own car and followed her out onto the street. Usually, he had her text one of them to make sure she arrived home safely, but despite everything she'd said, he knew something was wrong and he needed answers. When they reached her house, he sensed her nervousness and his anxiety went up a notch. He carried her bag inside and set it on a chair in her living room.

Raven kicked her shoes off and dropped down on the sofa. "I had fun, but I'm glad to be home. Oh, I'm sorry. You want something to drink or eat?"

Bryson sat next to her. "I'm good. So, what's going on?"

"Don't I get five minutes before you start in?"

"You had over a week, so spill it." His brows knit together. "You're not sick, are you?"

"No, Bryse, I'm not sick. Well, maybe I am. I'm sick of hooking up with losers."

"Darren?"

"Yeah." She buried her head in her hands. "Why does this keep happening?"

"Tell me about it," he said gently. He felt bad about her always finding losers, but didn't say it aloud.

"He wanted me to change my job."

"Excuse me?"

"He doesn't like that I work with athletes, so he suggested I take a job in a hospital or something because he's an insecure ass. We argued and he grabbed my arm, talking about I embarrassed him."

"He actually said that to you? And he put his hands on

you?" It took everything in Bryson to keep his seat and not find Darren and lay hands on *him*.

She nodded. "We went out to dinner and two of my clients—one former—were at the restaurant and came over to say hello. Darren barely acknowledged them and as soon as they left the table he asked if I had considered his suggestion. Do you know he went so far as to ask a friend of his about a position in a hospital? And had the nerve to tell me this guy wouldn't hold the position forever." She folded her arms. "As far as I'm concerned, he can hold it until hell freezes over." Tears filled her eyes.

"I honestly don't know what to say. I mean what man would ask his woman to change a job that she's worked so hard to get? I'm sorry, Raven."

"So am I." A tear escaped down her cheek and she quickly wiped it away. "I hate crying," she muttered.

Bryson's heart clenched. He couldn't handle her tears. He slid off the sofa, hunkered down in front of her and grasped both her hands. "Listen to me. You are an intelligent and beautiful woman, and you don't need to be with anyone who doesn't recognize your worth. Forget all about him."

"I don't think I can do this again," Raven cried. "It seems like every guy I meet wants me to change my job, my friends or both. Then there's that silly pact I made with Mackenzie, Ryleigh and Qui—" She cut herself off.

He'd met her childhood friends once when they'd visited a few years ago. They were a lively group of women. "What pact?"

She waved a hand and tried to stand. "It's nothing."

Bryson blocked her exit and stared at her, waiting.

"Fine. When we went home for Ava's wedding last year, Quinn talked us into making an agreement that we would all be married within a year. She's a serious romantic, but with my track record, I don't know what I was thinking. The crazy thing is Mac and Ryleigh, the last two people on earth we expected to do anything remotely permanent when it came to relationships, found great guys and are happily married."

He rose, reclaimed his seat and turned her face toward his. "I only met your friends once, so I can't speak to their relationships, but I promise you'll find someone worthy of you. Any man would be proud to have a woman like you by his side."

Raven palmed his face. "I don't know what I'd do without you, Bryse. You always know the right things to say." She placed a soft kiss on his cheek.

A shock of awareness shot through Bryson and he went still. *What the hell?* She'd touched and kissed him a million times, but tonight something felt different. He knew she'd felt it too when their eyes locked. Suddenly, the air around them thickened with sexual tension, something that had never happened before.

"Bryson," she whispered.

Without thought, he slanted his mouth over hers in a kiss that would have knocked him to his knees had he been standing.

"What…what are we doing?" she asked, a mixture of wonder and confusion in her voice.

"I believe it's called kissing. I'm kissing my best friend and…I think I want to do it again." When she offered no protest, he captured her lips again and experienced the same jolt. If they chose to proceed, he knew it would irrevocably change their relationship, but he couldn't stop. And he didn't *want* to.

# Chapter Three

Raven couldn't believe she was kissing her best friend. And boy could he kiss! In just one minute, Bryson had every molecule in her body on fire. She pulled back. Somewhere in the back of her mind, a voice said she should stop this before things went too far, but it was quickly drowned out by the rising passion between them. The kisses changed from sweet and tender to demanding and all-consuming.

"If you want me to stop, I need you to say something now. Tell me to stop, Raven."

She wrapped her arms around him. "I can't. I don't…don't stop."

Bryson searched her face. "Are you sure about this? I need you to be sure, baby because we won't be able to go back."

He'd never called her baby before and the sound of the endearment did something to her insides. "I'm sure. I need you, Bryse."

He swept her into his arms and strode down the hallway to her bedroom. He gently laid her on the bed and followed her down, placing kisses all over her face. "I need you to know that I will never hurt you, Raven."

This was unchartered territory for her and she was grateful for his assurance. She wouldn't know what to do if she lost his friendship. "Thank you for always being here for me."

"No thanks necessary," Bryson murmured, still gifting her

with kisses along her jaw. "You've done the same for me countless times. No matter what happens after today, I will still be here for you. Always."

Raven met his eyes and saw the truth in them. She smiled. When he smiled back, her pulse skipped. She reached up and pushed his locs back and kissed him.

He groaned. His hand roamed up her thigh, to her torso and higher still to her breast. "I think I'm going to like touching you almost as much as I'm coming to enjoy kissing you." He reclaimed her mouth.

She liked his kisses too, but no way could she answer. Not with his tongue swirling and teasing hers, sending shockwaves of pleasure through her. Her hands slid beneath his shirt and she traced a path from his rock-hard abs to his well-defined chest and arms. She knew he worked out regularly and kept himself in good shape, but she'd never contemplated how good it would feel to touch him this way. He trailed kisses down her exposed throat and chest, igniting a blaze along the way.

Bryson pulled her to a sitting position and removed her T-shirt. He ran his finger over the tops of her breasts then replaced it with his tongue. "You're beautiful, Raven. Why do you hide beneath the big shirts?"

"I...*ohhh.* I...don't..." Raven gave up trying to talk and let the sensations take over. He unhooked her bra and slowly dragged the straps down, and the heat of his gaze hardened her nipples instantly. He rubbed his thumbs over the sensitive peaks then circled his tongue around first one, then the other before suckling each one. She gasped sharply. She wanted him inside her now. "Bryson. *Now.*"

"Can't do that, sweetheart. You're my best friend and you're special to me. *This* is special to me and I'm going to spend each moment showing you how much."

His words touched a part of her heart she didn't know existed and heightened her arousal. "Bryse..."

"What, baby?"

"You're special to me, too." His hand feathered over her torso and lower until he reached the waistband of her shorts. With deft fingers, he released the button, lowered the zipper and slid them and her panties down, grazing her core. Raven moaned. His hand traveled down her left leg then back up her right leg and inner thigh. She parted her legs to give him better access and he took full advantage, stroking, circling and teasing her clit. Her legs trembled and she opened wider. Bryson then parted her folds and plunged one finger in, followed by another. She cried out and arched against his hand. He moved them in and out in a steady rhythm until she felt the pressure building.

"So damn beautiful," Bryson murmured, leaning up to kiss her.

Raven tore her mouth away and screamed as an orgasm slammed into her.

He withdrew, stood to remove his clothes and donned a condom.

Still trying to catch her breath, she let her gaze roam over Bryson's magnificent caramel-toned body—six-three height, slim muscular build, gorgeous face, whiskey-colored eyes and sexy locs. It was as if she were seeing him for the first time. She held her arms out to him and he lowered himself into her embrace. "You are a pure work of art," she whispered against his lips.

He chuckled. "I'm glad you think so." He slanted his mouth over hers once again. He nudged her legs apart and positioned himself at her entry. "Are you ready for this?"

She knew he meant more than just the sex. "Yes." Their eyes locked and they grew quiet, realizing that this was a turning point in their friendship and that there would be no going back after today. He guided himself inside, filling her until he was buried to the hilt.

For a moment he didn't move. "Raven, this…I can't explain it. It's…"

"I know. I feel it, too." The connection, something drawing

them together in a way that neither of them understood. He teased her with short strokes, then long, deep ones she felt all the way to her core. She locked her legs around his waist and her hands slid across his broad back, feeling his muscles flex and bunch as he thrust. He rotated his hips slowly, provocatively, delving deeper with each rhythmic push. The intense sensations spread throughout her body and electrified all her nerve endings.

Bryson gripped her hips and increased the tempo. "You feel so good, you make me never want to leave your body."

That made two of them. Her eyes slid closed. Their breathing grew louder as he pumped harder and faster, rocking the bed. Raven arched to meet his driving thrusts and tightened her legs around him. Bryson pulled out to the tip and surged back inside her. Her eyes flew open and she came in a rush of pleasure that wrenched his name from her throat and left her weak and dizzy. A heartbeat later, he joined her, shouting her name and shuddering deeply. They clung to each other as the aftershocks continued to rock their bodies.

Bryson braced himself on his forearms and stared down at her. He caressed her cheek then covered her mouth in a sweet, gentle kiss. He rolled to his side, cradled her in his arms and pressed a kiss to her forehead.

Raven laid her head on his chest and listened to the strong, steady beat of his heart. She thought she would feel some sense of regret and maybe she would tomorrow, but right now she only felt incredibly satisfied. A few minutes later, Bryson's breathing became deep and even. She lifted her head and observed him in his sleep. He possessed all the qualities a woman would look for in a man—amazing personality, loyal, had a good job, not to mention being handsome as all get out. So why hadn't some woman already claimed him? She searched her mind, trying to remember the last time he mentioned dating anyone, and came up blank. But, then again, she didn't expect him to tell her about every woman he went out with. So where did that leave them? Where did it leave *her*?

* * *

Hours later, Bryson awakened to find Raven sprawled half on top of him. Her dark brown hair half covered her face and spilled over his chest. He fingered the shoulder- length strands. She'd gotten highlights a few months ago and it looked good on her. He drew in a deep breath as his mind traveled back to what had transpired between them. Never in his wildest dreams could he have imagined what it would be like to touch and kiss Raven the way he had, and certainly not how would feel to make love to her. So, why now? In all the years they'd been friends, he hadn't flirted with her once and he had no clue how to explain what happened today. But now that they'd crossed the line, they couldn't revert back to being just friends. And he didn't want to.

Bryson glanced down at her peaceful expression. The emotional pull he'd felt with her was different from anything he'd ever experienced with a woman and he needed to know why. Maybe it was because of their close friendship, or something else. He had no idea. The only way to find out would be for them to explore this thing drawing them together. His stomach growled softly. He rolled his head in the direction of the clock on her nightstand and saw it was close to midnight. They'd been asleep for over five hours, far past dinner and his belly let him know that he needed to find some food soon.

He had a myriad emotions swirling around and desperately wanted to talk to Raven to find out if she felt the same, but they both had work in the morning. He and Jerome still had to finish the unpacking and he had a seven-thirty meeting with a potential business donor. With the bulk of the center's donations coming through grants from corporations such as this one, he couldn't afford to put the meeting off. The ten-thousand-dollar grant would go a long way to support the summer programs they wanted to put in place.

Sighing with regret, Bryson stroked a finger down her cheek and placed a soft kiss on her lips. "Wake up, sleepyhead." She pushed his hand away and kept sleeping. He chuckled and kissed her again while running his hand up and down her spine. "Raven, wake up. I need to leave."

Raven's eyes popped open. She gasped and tried to back away from him.

Bryson held on to her. "It's okay, baby."

She stared at him a moment then relaxed. "What time is it?"

"Almost midnight."

"I'm starving." She shifted and the sheet slid down, revealing her sable-tipped breasts.

He hardened immediately. He was starving, too, but now for something entirely different. Her gaze flew to his. She had to feel his growing erection pressing against her thigh. "Hey, you said you were starving and I'm more than ready to fill you up. But, I'm going to have to take a raincheck. I need to get going so I can get a few hours of sleep. I have a seven-thirty meeting."

Raven groaned. "I forgot I have to be at work at seven in the morning."

"At least you don't have to leave the warmth of your bed. You can turn over and go back to sleep."

She smiled. "Sorry."

"We need to talk, so I'll come by after you get off."

Her smile faded.

Bryson frowned. "What's the frown for? Are you having regrets?"

"No, but…" Raven sighed with exasperation. "I don't know. I just feel *weird*."

He totally understood because he was experiencing the same confusion. "And that's something we'll discuss." She still seemed uncertain and he sought to reassure her. "Everything will work out, but I want you to remember that what we shared was special to me. Okay?"

She nodded.

He captured her mouth, letting his kiss communicate what his words could not. He left the bed and dressed in the dark.

Raven found her T-shirt, slipped it on and followed him to the door to lock up.

"Text me and let me know what time you think you'll be home."

"Okay. Drive safe."

"I will. Good night."

Bryson made the drive from Long Beach to Manhattan Beach in less than half an hour. He showered and ate then headed to his bedroom. By the time he laid his head on the pillow, the clock read 1:00 a.m. Despite his body being tired, his mind raced and he had a hard time falling asleep.

When the alarm went off at five thirty, Bryson felt like he hadn't slept at all. He dragged himself out of bed and got ready for work. Most days, he didn't wear a suit, but today he chose a navy one and paired it with a white dress shirt and his favorite matching patterned tie. He packed a pair of jeans and tee to change into after the meeting.

He didn't drink coffee every morning, but today he needed it strong and black. Hefting his duffle and laptop bag on his shoulder, he picked up his coffee and made his way to the garage. Bryson depressed the wall switch and the door rose. He placed the bags in the backseat, hung his suit coat on the hook then slid in on the driver's side.

The drive to his Torrance community center took only fifteen minutes. In his office, he stuck in his flash drive and opened his presentation. He took the laptop down to the small conference room they used for meetings and connected it to the projector. He went through each slide to make sure they were in order.

"Morning."

He looked up at Jerome's entrance. "Morning."

"Everything ready?" Jerome propped a hip on the edge of the table.

"Yep."

"You were supposed to call me after you talked to Raven.

What happened?"

Bryson couldn't begin to describe what happened. "I'll tell you about it later."

He angled his head. "Is she okay? Was it Darren?"

"It was him. He wanted her to change jobs because he's concerned that one of the athletes she works with is going to flirt with her."

"You're kidding me, right?"

He shook his head and stood. "No, I'm not. So she gave him the boot."

"She must've been really upset last night since you didn't call."

A memory of Raven's sounds of pleasure while they made love last night rang in his ears.

Jerome eyed him. "What's going on?"

He ran a hand over his locs. "Like I said, we'll talk later." Bryson didn't really want to share what went on with him and Raven because she might be uncomfortable around them if they knew. But since he planned for them to begin seeing each other, Jerome and Kendrick would know something had changed five seconds after seeing them together. For the first time, Bryson wondered what the two men would think about him and Raven dating.

"Morning, guys."

He and Jerome turned at the sound of the administrative assistant's voice. "Good morning, Tonya." He'd hired Tonya Franklin shortly after opening the center. After having back surgery, the forty-something-year-old woman couldn't return to her former position as a preschool teacher because of the physical nature of the job. Bryson had purchased a sit-stand work station that allowed her to change her position as often as she needed and had given her a flexible work schedule.

"Morning, Ms. T," Jerome said.

"The camping trip was successful?"

"It was. And Jerome embarrassed himself trying to do a

dance-off with the kids."

"I did not get embarrassed," Jerome said with mock indignation. "I'll have you know, I can hang with them any day."

Tonya burst out laughing. "I sure wish I could've seen that."

Bryson chuckled. "You can. I recorded every second."

Jerome's eyes widened. "What?"

"You honestly didn't think I'd let that priceless moment pass. I may need some leverage."

"You two are a mess. Bryson, do you need anything for your meeting?"

"No, I have everything ready."

"Okay. Holler if you need me."

After she was gone, Jerome shook his head. "I can't believe you recorded it. Just wrong, man."

"I didn't upload it to social media, so…" He shrugged and sauntered out of the room.

Jerome followed. "If I see that video anywhere near Facebook, Twitter, Instagram, LinkedIn, Snapchat or any other form of social media, I'm gonna kick your ass."

Bryson merely smiled and kept going until he reached his office.

"I mean it, Bryse." Jerome folded his arms and glared.

"You said you weren't embarrassed, so what's the problem?" He leafed through the contents of the folder and, satisfied it had all the information he wanted to pass along, closed it. "Relax. You know how I feel about posting personal stuff."

Tonya stuck her head in the door. "Mr. Walters is here. Do you want me to escort him to the conference room?"

"Yes, please." Bryson turned to Jerome. "Well, let's get this show on the road." He slipped into his suit coat, picked up the folder and retraced his steps to the conference room. "Mr. Walters, I'm Bryson Montgomery. Thank you for coming," he said, extending his hand. He'd been expecting someone older, but the slender blond-haired man looked to be around Bryson's age.

"Nice to meet you, Bryson. Call me Garrett."

He nodded. "This is my partner, Jerome Smith."

The two men exchanged greetings and shook hands.

He had planned to offer him coffee, but Tonya had it covered. "I know your time is valuable so we'll get started."

Jerome began with the vision of the center, the services they currently offered and their future goals. "We'd like to add two full-time staff members for the summer school program, as well as institute a health clinic once a month."

Garrett nodded. "What kinds of things will you teach?"

"Math and English, along with doing science projects and providing life skills training for high school juniors and seniors."

Bryson took over and shared statistics from before and after the center's founding, the positive impact it had made on the students, school and community. He also talked about the increased parental involvement over the past two years. When he finished, he answered the detailed questions Garrett asked without missing a beat. This was his baby and he knew it inside and out.

"I'm very impressed with your program, Bryson. You and Jerome seem to be filling a void in the community that's sorely needed. We were prepared to give you a ten-thousand-dollar grant, but the board has given me permission to change those numbers a bit." Garrett took out a checkbook and started writing.

Bryson and Jerome shared a look. Was he going to give them less? Bryson didn't realize he'd been holding his breath until he felt the tightness in his chest. He hesitantly accepted the check. When he saw the amount, he wanted to shout, but kept his composure. "Thank you, Garrett. This is very generous." He passed it to Jerome, whose eyes widened for a split second before he caught himself.

"We're always looking for good programs to support and yours has a reputation for being honest and productive. Do you have any materials I can take back and pass along to some of my business friends?"

Jerome handed him the folder. "This contains brochures about our programs and goals, as well as a wish list."

"Great. Thank you."

"We appreciate your donation."

Garrett reached out to shake their hands. "I won't take up any more of your time."

"I'll walk you out," Jerome said.

Jerome came back as Bryson finished shutting down the laptop and they let out a loud whoop. "I can't believe they gave us five times the amount of the grant." Bryson picked up the check again to make sure the numbers were correct.

"Man, that's more than enough to pay the stipend for two teachers for the six-week program. And aren't the new laptops supposed to be delivered sometime next week?"

"And do several other things. Yes to the laptops." They had already interviewed the teachers in hopes that the grant would come through. There was money available, but it had been earmarked for other projects down the road and he hadn't wanted to dip into it. His cell vibrated. He pulled it out of his pocket and smiled upon seeing Raven's name on the display. He read her text letting him know what time she would be home and sent a reply.

"Why are you smiling?"

"That was Raven."

Jerome closed the door. "You were going to tell me what happened with her."

"She was talking and crying, then things got a little complicated."

"What does that mean?"

Bryson paused a beat. "We slept together."

For a moment, Jerome stared in shock then anger clouded his features. "You *what*?" he yelled. "Dammit, Bryse! You were supposed to be helping her, not helping yourself to her—"

"Don't!" He pinned him with a lethal glare. "It wasn't like that," he said through gritted teeth. "And you know I would never just casually do something like that with her."

Jerome paced back and forth.

"Rome, I don't need you giving me grief over this. Do you know how confusing this is for both of us? We've been friends all this time and not once did I look at her in that way."

"Then what happened yesterday?"

Bryson dropped down in a chair and scrubbed a hand down his face. "I wish I knew. She was telling me about what Darren did and I consoled her like we always do. Then she touched me and I felt something different. I think she felt it, too. It shocked us both."

"You couldn't just walk away?" Jerome asked sarcastically.

"No. I don't believe she could, either. I'm telling you it was weird. It seemed like something was pulling us, something we couldn't control." Even now, he recalled that moment, and he no more understood it today than he did yesterday.

"So what are you going to do?"

Before Bryson could answer, a knock sounded. Jerome, standing closest to the door opened it.

"What's up?" Kendrick asked, coming in with a huge grin.

He lowered his head to the desk and groaned. Now he would have to hear the same spiel again.

"I figured since I have all this wonderful time on my hands, I'd come and help you guys put away everything from the camping trip." He divided a speculative glance between Jerome and Bryson. "Did something happen? Is it Raven? You found out why she'd been crying?"

"Ask Bryse."

Kendrick looked to Bryson for answers.

"Yes, I found out." Bryson groaned again. "And she and I slept together yesterday."

"You *what?*"

He repeated the same thing he told Jerome. "We're going to talk tonight. I want to see where this goes, but I don't know how she feels."

Kendrick braced his hands on the table. "Bryse, do you

realize what'll happen if you break her heart? We will kill you. Raven is special. She's like a sister. We're supposed to be taking care of her, not…not…" He threw up his hands.

"I am *not* going to break her heart," he gritted out and slammed his hand on the table. "She's just as special to me, if not more." He jumped to his feet and stalked toward the door. He was angry that they would think he'd hurt Raven.

Jerome stepped into his path and placed a staying hand on his chest. "Look, Bryse. Let's all calm down. I think we're just shocked. We know you wouldn't do anything to hurt Raven, but if things don't work out between you two, it's going to be pretty awkward."

He released a long breath. "You don't think I know that? It scares the hell out of me that I might hurt her, but I *have* to see this through. What I experienced with her was different than with any other woman and I need to know why. I also need you guys to trust that I wouldn't do anything that might cause her pain. She's been through enough." Bryson took a moment to fill Kendrick in on the details of what occurred with Darren.

"What an ass. Maybe she would be better off with you."

"Don't say anything to Raven about what I just told you for now. I don't want her to feel awkward around you."

"We're supposed to do dinner on Friday," Kendrick reminded him.

"Hopefully, she and I will have come to an agreement on how to proceed." The only acceptable answer in Bryson's mind was that they'd start dating. He just needed to convince Raven.

# Chapter Four

Monday morning, Raven could barely keep her eyes open. She stifled a yawn as she sat at the computer entering the chart information on her last two clients. The ramifications of what she'd done had hit her hard as soon as she woke up. She still didn't regret one moment with Bryson, but she was in a strange place that she couldn't define. She started to send him a text earlier to let him know what time she planned to be home, but got cold feet about talking to him.

Setting aside thoughts of Bryson, she went out to greet her next client. One of the therapists had called in sick and the other therapists were covering, which, thankfully, left little time for her to think about her predicament. Raven had back-to-back clients for the next four hours and barely had enough time to stop and eat. They had started staggering the lunches a year ago, instead of closing the office for an hour. It usually wasn't a problem until someone was out, like today. She hurriedly ate her sandwich and carrots, finishing just in time for her new client, a sixty-four-year-old woman who'd had back surgery. During the evaluation, the woman chatted away about the good and bad of her forty-year marriage, bringing to mind Raven and Bryson's encounter. Again.

Despite her busy schedule, Raven's thoughts kept straying to Bryson and the intense passion they'd shared. She had finally sent the text, but still had trouble reconciling their encounter. In the back of her mind, she speculated on how this would impact their friendship. She didn't know what she'd do if she lost him. She felt her phone buzz in her pocket, but didn't stop what she was doing to check it. Somehow, she knew she would see Bryson's name on the display. Then there was Jerome and Kendrick. What would they think? She sighed inwardly and tried to refocus on the task in front of her.

Raven wanted to shout "Hallelujah!" when her day ended. On the way to the car, she checked her cell and saw the message from Bryson: *Hope your day is going well. Looking forward to seeing you later.* Any other time, his words wouldn't have caused a blip on her radar, but today it was going off like Fourth of July fireworks. He seemed anxious to talk to her. Did he have regrets or think they'd made a mistake? Although she hadn't seen him with another woman, it didn't mean he wasn't casually seeing one. No, he wouldn't have slept with her while dating someone else. She got into her car and leaned her head back. She was making herself crazy and needed to get a grip. She'd never been one to get all emotional and this, along with the amount of crying she had done over the past few weeks was ruining her tough girl image.

Merging into the nightmare traffic, Raven hit the *play* button on her iPod and let the sounds of Jaheim take her home. She wasn't surprised to see Bryson pulling into the condo complex behind her. He parked in a nearby visitor's spot and came to help her out of the car.

"Hey." Bryson gave her a warm hug.

"Hey." She led the way to her unit and let them in. "Have a seat." Raven didn't know how to behave around him right now.

He seemed to sense it because he took her hand and led her to the sofa. "You're worried, I can tell. Let's talk, sweetheart."

She flopped back against the sofa. "I don't know what's going on with me. One minute, I'm okay with us, the next, I'm not so sure. I feel uncomfortable, awkward and," she rolled her head in his direction, "afraid that I'm going to lose my best friend."

Bryson leaned forward, braced his forearms on his thighs

and clasped his hands together. "I get where you're coming from Raven, but I don't want you to feel any of those things. Nothing has changed. You're still my very best friend and always will be, no matter what."

"You say that today, but what if two weeks from now, you decide we don't work or you find someone else? Regardless of what you think, things *will* change between us."

He shifted to face her. "The only thing I'm going to want two weeks from now is to continue seeing my best friend."

Raven sat up straight and searched his face. "What are you talking about, Bryse?"

He reached for her hand and brought it to his lips. "I'm talking about you and me seeing where this goes, taking things one step at a time and exploring what I know we both are feeling."

"Bryse, I…I don't know." This was the last thing she expected him to say. She figured he'd either say they should go back to being friends or maybe friends with occasional benefits, but dating exclusively never crossed her mind.

"Tell me you don't feel the same connection, the same pull and we'll go back to the way it was before yesterday."

She couldn't say it because she did feel it, and it drew her like no other.

"Raven, I know this is scary. For both of us. But I think we'd regret it if we didn't find out for sure."

Raven stood and paced the living room. She couldn't think with him touching her and staring at her with those eyes. She still didn't understand how, after twelve years, they had gotten to this place.

Bryson came and placed his hands on her shoulders. "You're going to wear a hole in this carpet. And since you're leasing the place, I don't think you want to have to replace it," he added with a smile. "Let me ask you something."

She stared up at him. He towered over her five-six height by a good nine inches. "What?"

"Have I ever done anything to hurt you?"

"No."

"And have I ever given you any reason to doubt my word?"

"No."

"I won't start now." He placed a kiss on her forehead.

"I believe you. I'm going to change, I'll be right back."

He nodded and released her.

She needed a moment to process this and make some decisions. Things were moving at warp speed and, although she had some lingering reservations, she trusted Bryson with her life.

* * *

Bryson watched her walk away and wanted to call her back, take her into his arms and assure her that everything would work out. He lowered himself back to the sofa. She'd always been strong and outspoken. He'd only seen glimpses of vulnerability during her breakups, but even then, they had been short-lived and she would be back to her tough-as-nails self in a day or two. But this time seemed to be different and he didn't know how to make her see that he would never turn his back on her. Sure, he'd be disappointed if sometime down the road things didn't work out. However, being friends first, he hoped they would be able to mutually agree to remain close. Bryson chuckled to himself. After all this time, it would be ironic if Raven turned out to be the *one* Kendrick talked about.

He rose to his feet when Raven came back with two bottles of water. She had changed out of her slacks and polo emblazoned with the rehab center's logo into an oversized tee and shorts, and her feet were bare. His gaze was riveted to her toned, long legs. Memories of them wrapped around his waist as he thrust into her surfaced in his mind, and he felt himself growing hard. He wanted a repeat of last night so badly it hurt, but Raven needed time to get used to them as a couple. She still appeared somewhat apprehensive, but the frightened look he'd seen in her eyes a few minutes ago had disappeared.

Raven held out one bottle. "I figured you'd want one." She

sat in her same spot and tucked her feet under her.

Smiling, he accepted it from her, twisted off the cap and took a long drink, hoping it would cool his raging libido. "You figured right." His expression turned serious. "How're you doing with this? I know you needed a few minutes."

She halted with the bottle halfway to her lips. "How did you know?"

"Because I know you," Bryson said, reclaiming his seat. "What can I do to make this easier for you?"

"I don't know that there's anything you can do, but I'd trust you with my life, Bryson, so I'm willing to do as you suggested and take it one step at a time."

He read her message loud and clear—she trusted him not only with her life, but also her heart—and he vowed to do everything in his power to make sure she didn't regret her decision.

"Um…what do we tell Jerome and Kendrick?"

"The truth. They sort of already know," he said with a sheepish grin.

Her eyes widened. "You told them?"

"Only because I had to explain to Jerome why I didn't call him yesterday to let him know how you were doing. We all were worried about you. Kendrick showed up at the center at the tail end of the conversation, so…"

"And?" she prompted when he didn't continue.

"They lit into me because they thought I'd taken advantage of you, then threatened to kill me if I broke your heart."

Raven instinctively reached for his hand. "You've been friends with them longer. I don't want this to come between you guys."

"This won't affect our friendship, so don't start worrying. Once they saw how serious I was about you, they calmed down. I guess they're cool with it. We'll find out on Friday when we go out to dinner. Speaking of dinner, you want to grab a bite?"

She lifted a brow. "As long as I don't have to change, fine."

Bryson laughed. "Now, *that's* my girl." He'd been wanting

to kiss her from the moment he helped her out of the car and when she smiled at him, he couldn't hold back any longer. He leaned forward and brushed his lips across hers. When she didn't back away, he teased her bottom lip with his tongue and cupped the back of her head to bring her closer. Her lips parted and he slid his tongue into her mouth, reacquainting himself with her taste. Just like their first kiss, she didn't waste anytime reciprocating. He could feel his control slipping and eased back.

Raven moaned in protest.

"We need to slow down. Otherwise, we're going to end up back in your bed. We're supposed to be taking our time."

"I know, but when you kiss me, I don't want to stop."

Her confession made his heart leap. "Just so you'll know, it's the same with me." Most men wouldn't admit to something like that, but he wasn't like most men and he didn't want Raven to think for one moment that this was going to be a one-sided affair. "Get your shoes, so we can go. What do you have a taste for?"

She uncurled her legs. "I want a cheeseburger and french fries." She pointed a finger his way. "And don't say anything. I missed dinner last night and didn't have time to finish my lunch today, so I'm starving."

"I'm not saying anything." Bryson chuckled as she sashayed out.

They ended up at MVP Grill—where all of the entrées were named after sports figures—and decided to eat there.

As soon as the server brought their food, Raven said a quick blessing and bit into her burger. She moaned.

Bryson sucked in a sharp breath. He bowed his head and, along with his blessing, prayed he'd be able to go as slow as she needed.

"How did your meeting go this morning? I hope you got the grant."

He grinned. "We did, but instead of the ten thousand listed, he cut us a check for fifty thousand."

Raven gasped. "Are you serious? That is *fantastic*! Congratulations, Bryse. You and Jerome deserve it."

"Thanks. We're pretty excited because it gives us some breathing room."

"And you don't have to dip into your savings like I know you did last year," she said casually and popped a fry into her mouth.

Bryson didn't comment. He and Jerome received a decent salary from the board, but it was less than his previous job. Fortunately, he'd learned to save from an early age and had made investments that afforded him the ability to supplement the monies received for the center, if necessary.

"What plans do you have for the money?"

"So far, just hiring the teachers for the summer school program. Ken's going to volunteer, too, which means we only need two. Tonya suggested adding a preschool at some point, but we'll see."

"If you did, you wouldn't have to worry about hiring someone to develop and run the program."

He finished chewing and took a sip of his lemonade. "True. But we'd still need teachers year-round."

"What about having one or two permanent teachers and hiring college students majoring in Early Childhood Education as assistants. It would be a cheaper alternative."

Bryson studied her. "I hadn't thought about that." And with their non-profit status, they'd be eligible for more grants. The tuition collected would go back into the program, minimizing the impact on monies directed elsewhere. He nodded. "I like it. I'll talk to Rome about it tomorrow." They ate in silence for a few minutes. "How was your day? You mentioned having to go in early. I thought Friday was your early day."

"It is, but one of my clients is going out of town this week and needed to reschedule, so I went in early to accommodate him. It ended up being crazy busy because one of the therapists called in sick. Instead of canceling her appointments, we doubled up."

"No wonder you didn't get a chance to eat." Her food was gone. "I guess you were hungry."

Raven smiled. "Yeah, and this hit the spot. I'm going to have to do an extra day of working out, though."

"Trust me, everything is tight, toned and in all the right places."

She angled her head. "You flirting with me is going to take some getting used to." She stood. "Let's go."

"Well, you'd better hurry up because I'm going to be doing more than flirting." Bryson tossed her a bold wink and led her out to the car.

Once they got back to her place, Raven immediately kicked off her shoes, as usual, and curled up in her favorite position on the sofa. "I have a question and you can answer or not."

"What is it?"

"Why haven't you gotten serious about some woman before? I mean, look at you." She waved a hand in his direction. "You're smart, good-looking and in the dictionary next to the definition of a 'good Black man' is your picture."

He chuckled. "Ah, okay. I wouldn't go that far. Seriously? My picture in the dictionary. Hmm, that would be something." He laughed again.

She threw a pillow at him. "You know what I mean."

"I do. I guess I haven't really been looking, especially after what happened with Delaney."

"That wasn't your fault."

"I realize that. It took me a long time to understand she needed help. I just wished she'd confided in me." He dated Delaney for close to two years and thought she'd be the one he would marry after they graduated. During their junior year, she changed her major from Justice Studies to Nursing, something her family hadn't been happy about. What he didn't know, initially, was that they'd pressured her and threatened to cut off their financial support if she didn't follow through with what they wanted her to do. Her parents had both been attorneys and wanted her and her younger brother to join the family practice. Delaney started to withdraw and Bryson had tried to encourage her as much as he could, but she became depressed. In an effort to cheer her up, he planned a night out for them. When he arrived at her dorm room, he found her unconscious and barely alive with an empty bottle of sleep medication next to her. She died on the way to the hospital. Three days later, he received the letter she'd mailed, telling him she was sorry, but couldn't take the pressure anymore. He'd been angry and devastated. After that, he dated, but never got close to another woman.

"And now?"

Bryson scooped her up and settled her across his lap. "Now there's you and I can't help but to be serious."

"Because of our friendship?"

"No. Because of the way you make me feel." He lowered his head and kissed her. He liked the way she fit in his arms, the way her mouth fit against his, as if it had been created especially for him. When the kiss ended, he shifted until he was lying on his back and cradled Raven in his arms. They lay together without speaking for a long while and Bryson couldn't remember the last time he'd been so content. At length, he asked, "Do you have a long day tomorrow?"

"Not really." Raven laughed softly. "I have to deal with Chris and his antics, but other than that, it should go pretty smoothly."

"The football player who injured his back last season."

"The one and only. He keeps everybody cracking up."

"Is he the same one who came to the restaurant when you were out with Darren?"

"Yep. He told Darren he was a lucky guy because I had the best hands in the business."

Bryson chuckled. "I guess that didn't go over well. Can't say I'd want to be told by some rich football player that my woman has the best hands," he teased.

She elbowed him.

"I'm just sayin'."

"Are you going to be the same way?"

"No, baby. I have no reason not to trust you." He picked up one of her hands. "Besides, when word gets out about these hands, other athletes are going to be knocking on your door and, with your newfound celebrity status, you might be able to open your own clinic, if you want."

"Hmm…maybe sometime down the line. I see how hard you have to work and all the hours you put in, and I don't know if I want to commit to all that. As it stands, I hate having to chart and write reports, so I know I wouldn't want to have to do everything you do to run the center. Nah, I'll just go to work and come home. I like my sleep."

Bryson laughed. "Girl, you are a mess. I hear you on the workload, but I gotta tell you, I love being my own boss. If you ever decide you want to do it, you know I'll do everything to help you."

Without lifting her head from his chest, Raven reached up and patted his cheek. "Mmm hmm, baby, you go right ahead and be the boss."

He stilled. It was the first time she'd ever called him anything other than Bryson or Bryse. Her calling him *baby* went straight to his heart.

She slowly lifted her head. "What?"

"Nothing. I'm just enjoying being here with you."

"Me, too."

Smiling, he held her closer, thinking he could do this for a lifetime. Though the thought should have scared him as it usually did, this time he actually felt a measure of peace. And for a brief moment, he imagined what it would be like to come home to her everyday and lay just like this.

# Chapter Five

By Friday, Raven was only slightly more comfortable with her new relationship. However, she couldn't deny the growing feelings she had for Bryson. She'd dated Darren for four months and liked him reasonably well, but what she felt for Bryson surpassed those emotions tenfold and in a short time. He made it easy to fall for him, from not being threatened by her clients to suggesting she might want to open her own clinic someday and offering to help. So far, nothing about their easygoing relationship had changed and she wanted to believe that what they had would continue to grow. But she was a realist and if her track record was any indication, she didn't hold out much hope.

While Jerome and Kendrick knew, she hadn't mentioned it to her girlfriends or brother, Simeon, who was in Rosewood Heights visiting their parents. Raven was older by two years, but he often acted if their ages were reversed. He was due back next week and, although he knew Bryson, she didn't look forward to the interrogation that was sure to come. Her attorney brother would question her like he would a hostile witness on the stand.

Through the office window, she saw Mrs. Butler pass. The woman waved enthusiastically. Raven chuckled inwardly and waved back. Pushing back from her desk, she walked out to greet the woman. Maybe Raven could get through the session without her suggesting places where she might meet a "nice young man."

After the session ended, Raven completed her charting and

sent a text to her cousin, Erika to make sure they were still on for lunch. While Raven's mother had elected to stay in Rosewood Heights, her older sister—Erika's mother—had left to attend college and moved to LA after marrying her college sweetheart. Knowing she had family in the area had given Raven one more reason to attend college in the city.

Erika had injured her knee and, after being referred to the clinic for therapy, had her first appointment that afternoon. The two cousins hadn't talked in a few weeks and this would give them a chance to catch up.

Raven spotted Erika in the waiting room an hour later and mouthed that she'd be out in five minutes. She finished the progress note that would be sent to her client's doctor and logged off. She retrieved her purse from the locked drawer and slung it on her shoulder. "David, I'm going to lunch."

"Okay," he called over his shoulder.

Out front, she greeted Erika with a hug. "It's good to see you, cuz." Erika was three years older and often filled the role of an older sister.

"Ditto," Erika said. "You're looking good, girl."

They pushed through the front door. "I'll drive."

Erika limped down the ramp. "That's fine with me."

Raven pointed out her charcoal gray Acura and slowed her steps to match her cousin's.

Once in the car, she collapsed against the seat. "I can't believe how much having a knee issue tires me out."

"Well—"

"Don't start, Dr. Holloway. I do not need to know the science behind the whys. I just need it to be fixed."

"Whatever you say." From the moment Raven stepped across the stage with her clinical doctorate, Erika had taken to calling her that.

"Where are we going?"

"Just to a sandwich shop down the street on Sepulveda,"

she said, merging onto the street. The rehab clinic was located a few miles northeast of LAX. "How's Emery?"

"My hubby is doing well. He just got back from an emergency medicine conference in Philadelphia last week." The two had met at the hospital where they both worked—Emery as an emergency room physician and Erika as a nurse manager. "We're planning to do a Fourth of July barbeque, so put it on your calendar. You can bring Darren."

"Darren and I are not together anymore."

Erika turned in her seat. "I thought you two were getting along well."

A car pulled out of a parking spot near the sandwich shop just as she drove up and Raven quickly snagged it. "Things changed. I'll tell you about it while we eat."

Once they were seated with their food, Erika said, "Okay, I'm waiting. What happened?"

She told her about the dinner, his announcement about wanting to take things to the next level and the interruption by her clients. "After they left the table, Darren asked me if I had given his suggestion about changing my job more thought. He wanted me to work in a place where he wouldn't have to be concerned about my clients flirting, like a nursing home."

"Girl, I would've cussed him out, restaurant or not."

"I should have. I was so mad I told him to take me home and to not call me again. I ended up taking a cab after he tried to grab me."

She shook her head and bit into her sandwich.

"But that's not all. There's something else I wanted to talk about that's confusing me."

"Okay."

"I…Bryson and I slept together."

Erika started coughing. "You what? I thought this was going to be about Darren."

"No, Bryson."

"As in Bryson, your best friend?"

Raven nodded.

Erika leaned back in her chair and didn't say anything for a lengthy minute. "Wow. *Oo-kay*, so how did you end up, you know?"

"I was telling him about what happened with Darren and crying. One minute he's consoling me like he's always done and the next we're in my bed. It was crazy."

"I'll say."

"Seriously. I'd never felt anything for him outside of friendship, but that night I felt this strange *thing* when he touched me and when he kissed me, I didn't want him to stop."

"Honey, do you think it was just a rebound kind of thing? You were upset about the breakup with Darren. Bryson was just there at the right time when you were vulnerable."

"No. That's the one thing I'm sure about. I'd been with Darren for four months and he didn't make me feel any of the emotions I experienced with Bryse." Raven had asked herself the same thing and easily ruled it out.

"So, this was just one night of sex?"

She ate a chip.

"Raven?"

She shook her head. "We're sort of seeing each other now."

Erika picked up her drink and took a sip. She waved the cup. "You should've told me we were going to have this kind of conversation. I think I need something stronger than green tea. I take it that was his suggestion and not yours."

"Yes. How do you know?"

"You sound unsure. I remember Bryson being a pretty great guy, as well as his two friends. That hasn't changed, has it?"

"Not at all, but it just feels odd to say I'm dating my best friend."

"I get that. After it was over, did he get up and go home right after?"

"No. Why?"

Erika smiled. "So did he make eye contact with you during, cuddle with you after or kiss you on the forehead?"

Raven had no idea what she was getting at, but said, "Actually, he did all of them."

"*Yes!*" She slapped a hand over her mouth when a couple people turned around. "Girl, that means it was more than just sex to him. He might be a keeper."

Her brows knit in confusion. "What does that have to do with anything?"

Erika shook her head with exasperation. "If you weren't always such a tomboy, you'd know these things. Those are acts of intimacy and men don't do that kind of thing unless they're really into a woman."

Raven waved her off. "I need you to stop watching all those women's shows."

"You don't believe me? Okay, tell me this. If you slept with Darren, did he do the same thing?"

They'd only slept together a few times and in each instance, he'd gotten up almost immediately after, dressed and left like she had been nothing more than a booty call.

Erika smiled knowingly. "That look on your face says things were very different. Mark my words, Bryson is thinking serious relationship and I hope you're ready."

Her stomach knotted and she put her sandwich down. The smile on her cousin's face set off warning bells in Raven's head. Every serious relationship she'd had ended with her heart being ripped to pieces and she wouldn't be able to handle it if that were to happen with her and Bryson.

"Don't worry, love is a beautiful thing." She smiled and picked up her sandwich.

*Love?* All of a sudden, Raven felt lightheaded. They weren't in love. They'd only agreed to date less than a week ago. Her appetite now gone, she rewrapped her sandwich.

"You're not going to finish your food?"

"I'll eat it later."

Erika, on the other hand, had no problems demolishing her sandwich. "That was good. Now, I'm ready to get my therapy on."

Raven shook her head and smiled. "Let's go, crazy woman." As they walked back to the car, she asked, "Did you bring a pair of shorts?"

"No. What's wrong with my sweat pants? I'm just going to be doing some little exercises, right?"

"Erika, didn't you read the instructions? For your first appointment, they'll do an evaluation—check swelling, flexibility, range of motion. They can't see your knee in those, so you'll have to put on a hospital gown."

She cursed and got into the car. "I need some lotion. And don't say one word." She held up a hand. "Not, one word." Erika had a habit of not putting on lotion when she wore long pants.

Raven bit her lip to keep from laughing, but failed miserably. She dug into her purse, found a small tube of hand cream and handed it to her. "This is all I have."

Erika glared at Raven and snatched the tube out of her hand.

She figured Erika would wait until they got back to the clinic to put on the lotion, but Raven should have known better. The woman tried to put the lotion on while wearing her sweats. Raven burst out laughing at the comical picture she made sliding around on the seat while reaching inside her pants to lotion her thighs. When she pulled up her pant leg, Raven asked, "When was the last time you saw some lotion, girl? I've seen alligators with smoother skin."

"Shut up. I told you not to say a word."

Raven thought she was going to hurt herself from laughing so hard.

"You need to pay attention to the road, instead of cackling over there."

Raven could barely catch her breath. She wiped tears of mirth from her eyes. "I'm so glad you're my cousin. I needed this laugh."

"Obviously," Erika muttered, rolling her eyes. But she was smiling.

When they got back to the clinic, she found a closer spot, so Erika wouldn't have to walk too far. "Hey, don't get mad at me. You should've read the instructions."

"Yeah, yeah, whatever."

Inside, they shared a hug. "Thanks for listening, Erika."

"You know I'm always here. And I'm glad I could provide you with some amusement. Oh, and don't forget what I told you abut Bryson."

Her smile faded. She doubted she'd be able to forget. That he might be looking for something serious both excited and frightened her. For now, however, she thought it best to just stick to the agreement and take it one day at a time.

* * *

Friday evening, Bryson, Raven, Jerome and Kendrick sat around the table at the sports grill laughing and talking. Bryson had wanted to pick Raven up so that they could arrive together, but she had texted him earlier, saying she would rather drive herself like always. He hadn't been happy, but didn't push the issue. Thankfully, the only seat available when she arrived had been next to him. Otherwise, he would have spent the entire evening trying to come up with a way to get next to her. She tried to pretend as if everything was the same, but he'd caught her more than once staring his way. She wanted to keep him in the friend zone and he was determined to be more. Bryson observed her laughing at something Kendrick said. Why had he never noticed that her dark brown eyes sparkled whenever she laughed and why did the sound make his heart beat a little faster?

Raven held up her glass of beer. "I think we should have a toast to congratulate Bryse and Rome on the grant they received this week."

Everyone raised their glasses and Kendrick said, "To Bryse and Rome. May this be the first of many grants. Wishing you much success, my brothers." They all touched glasses and sipped.

Jerome set his glass down. “We just found out that the grant is renewable. We may only get the stated amount, but I’m cool with that.”

“Since you’re rolling in the dough, I shouldn’t have to donate my services. Here’s to a summer stipend,” Kendrick said with a chuckle.

Bryson snorted. “Nah, bro. Volunteering would look so much better when you decide to go into administration.”

Raven laughed and laid her hand on Bryson’s arm. “I have to agree. And, Ken, didn’t you say that we all should give back?”

Bryson shifted in his chair. Raven leaned against him and her hand on his arm played havoc with his body.

Jerome divided a glance between Bryson and Raven and smiled, as if he knew what Bryson was going through.

Bryson downed the rest of his beer and stood. “I’m going over to the pool table.”

“Raven, you want the first game?” Kendrick asked.

She glanced up at Bryson and hesitated briefly. “No, that’s okay. You can go ahead. I want to finish my food first.”

As soon as they were out of earshot, Kendrick said, “You’ve got it bad, man. When you first told me about you and Raven, I thought it was just a fluke, but you’re really feeling her, aren’t you?”

“I told you I was.”

“And Raven?”

“She’s getting used to the idea. I told her we’d go slowly. She’s worried about losing me as a friend and, although she hasn’t said so directly, I know she’s also thinking we won’t work out.” During their conversation about her previous breakup, she mentioned that her relationships never lasted.

He set up the game and took the first shot. “I hope it does. I’ve never seen you watch a woman the way you do her.” He shook his head and chuckled. “Wouldn’t it be something if the two of you ended up married?”

"It would." Bryson had wondered the same thing and the more he mulled it over in his mind, the more he began to warm up to the idea that Raven could be the one for him. She possessed all the qualities he wanted in a woman—intelligence, humor, beauty, a perfect partner in the bedroom—and he envisioned that there would never be a dull moment with her around. He glanced at her over his shoulder as she laughed and talked to Jerome.

"Are you playing or not?" Kendrick asked with amusement.

He turned back and stepped up to the table. "Shut up. You act like you didn't do the same thing when you and Sandra first started dating." He lined up his shot and sank the first ball. He walked around the table and missed the next one.

"What can I say? A beautiful woman will do that to you."

Bryson laughed. "So I'm finding out."

Halfway through the game, Jerome and Raven came over.

"I've got next," Raven said.

Kendrick sank his next two balls. "I'll be ready for you as soon as I'm done kicking Bryson's butt."

"Whatever, boy. Just take your shot and skip all the BS." Bryson was two shots from losing the game.

A moment later, Kendrick sent the eight ball flying into a corner pocket. "Like I said… Let's go, Raven."

Raven took the cue stick from Bryson. "Rack 'em up. And I hope you don't think you're going to do the same thing to me."

"Girl, you'd better recognize the king."

She snorted. "We'll see, so quit stalling."

"I'll even let you go first."

She batted her eyes and said sweetly, "Aw, thank you, Ken."

They all burst out laughing and Kendrick shook his head.

When she bent over the table, her slacks stretched taut over her backside and Bryson sucked in a sharp breath. In a way he was glad he'd lost. He wouldn't be able to concentrate on the game with her positioned like that for any length of time. It took all he had to stand there and not run his hands over the smooth, round globes. He wanted to slowly slide her slacks and panties down her legs and ease his—

"Yo, Bryse!" Jerome nudged him. "Man, what are you thinking about?"

"Just thinking about the grant," he lied. No way would he say what was really going on in his mind. His erection throbbed and he stepped behind a bar stool to hide the growing evidence of his desire. "Did you say something?"

"Yeah. I asked if you wanted another beer or something."

"I'll take a lemonade. Actually, I'll go get it. What do you guys want?" He took their orders and went to the bar for the drinks, hoping that by the time he returned his body would have calmed some. *What the hell is wrong with me?* This attraction to Raven had come out of nowhere and was now barreling down the tracks like a runaway train. He had to get a grip. Since they'd be leaving soon, all had opted for non-alcoholic drinks. Bryson returned with the drinks just as the game ended. He set the glasses on a small table.

"You have just been dethroned, Oh King," Raven crowed as she strutted around the table. "Bow to the queen."

Kendrick took her hand and did a sweeping bow. "I will be wanting a rematch, Miss Queen."

She waved a dismissive hand. "We'll see."

Bryson handed her a glass of iced tea. "To the queen."

They all raised their glasses and shouted, "To the queen."

Raven skewered them with a look. "Cut it out you nuts." She smiled.

Kendrick picked up his drink. "Anybody else want to play?"

"I think I'll sit this week out," Jerome said. "I don't want to knock Raven off her throne so soon after her victory."

She rolled her eyes. "In your dreams, Mr. Dance-A-Mania."

"You're a cold woman."

Bryson and Kendrick howled.

Once Bryson regained a semblance of control, he put his arm around Raven's shoulder and kissed her temple. "That was the best one of the night." While Jerome and Kendrick still laughed, Bryson leaned close to Raven's ear. "And when we leave, I'm going to give you your reward, my queen." He smiled down at her shocked expression. And with about twenty minutes of daylight still left, he knew exactly what he wanted to do.

# Chapter Six

Bryson followed Raven home from the sports bar. He got out and walked over to her car. "You want to take a ride with me?"

"Where are we going?"

"Just to the beach." The past couple of days had been warmer than usual, with temperatures near ninety. Now at eight, they'd cooled to the mid-seventies.

Raven stared at him as if contemplating his offer. "Sure. Let me change real quick."

"I'll wait for you in the car." If he went inside, they would not be leaving and he was trying to keep his promise to go slow.

"Okay."

He sat in the car listening to the latest Bruno Mars song and tapping out the rhythm on his steering wheel. She came back in a flash wearing a pair of denim crop pants and a fitted tee. "That was fast."

"You know I don't take forever to pick out clothes. I'm either wearing it or not."

Bryson chuckled and started the engine. He made the short five-minute drive and, with the late hour, easily found parking in the lot. The sun had just about gone down, but they had a few minutes to play a short game of volleyball. He popped the trunk, got out and retrieved the ball, and then came around to help her out.

"Volleyball?"

"Yep. We have enough light to play to ten. You in?"

Raven looked at him as if he'd asked a silly question. "Of course."

He bowed. "After you, Your Majesty."

She snatched the ball, rolled her eyes and strutted off.

Bryson chuckled and followed. They walked across the sand to the nearest net and removed their shoes.

She tossed him the ball. "You can go first, since this will be your only chance to serve."

He gave her a kiss and ducked under the net. He served and she returned it with the quickness and power of a professional athlete. He loved her competitive spirit. They went back and forth fairly evenly until the score was tied at nine.

"Looks like I'm about to be two for two tonight," Raven bragged, slightly winded.

She served it and Bryson ran up and slammed it slightly over the net on her side. She dove and just missed it. "Looks can be deceiving, baby."

Raven stood up and brushed the sand off her clothes. "Yeah, well next time."

He crossed the net. "I think I deserve a reward for winning. And I owe you for the pool game." He brushed her hair off her face. "And I know the perfect prize," he said as he lowered his head and pulled her closer. He'd been waiting all evening to hold her in his arms and kiss her this way. His hands journeyed up her spine and to her shoulders. He cradled her face between his hands and brushed his lips across her cheeks, her forehead and her closed eyelids before reclaiming her mouth. She came up on her tiptoes, slid her hands around his back under his shirt and pressed her body against his, eliciting a groan from his throat. He lifted his head.

"What are you doing to me?" she whispered.

"The same thing you're doing to me."

She stepped out of his embrace and walked toward the water.

Bryson gave her a minute then followed. He fit himself behind her and wrapped his arms around her. "Are you still having trouble with this?"

"Yes…no…I don't know. You've always been in the friend zone and now that you're out—"

"Now that I'm out, I can't see going back to that exclusively."

"And I don't want that, either. I wasn't sure how to act around Rome and Ken tonight at first with them knowing about us."

Bryson had picked up on her hesitancy when she first arrived, but as the evening progressed, she had relaxed. "Did either of them say anything to you?"

"No. Did they say anything to you?"

"Kendrick noticed how hard it was for me to take my eyes off you and he said he hoped it worked out." He thought it best to skip the part about her being the one for now. "You seemed to be okay after a while."

"Yeah." The breeze kicked up and she shivered.

"We can leave if you're cold."

Raven angled her head. "Can we sit for a few minutes?"

He answered by lowering himself to the sand and pulling her down next to him. After a minute or two of silence, they talked about everything and nothing and Bryson marveled at the fact that after so many years of friendship, they never ran out of things to say. Their conversation had a natural flow and the relaxed camaraderie they shared was something he treasured. He grasped her hand and they listened to the waves crashing against the shore as the gentle breeze blew. "What are you doing tomorrow night?"

"I don't have anything planned."

"I'd like to take you out to dinner. Is seven a good time?"

"Yes."

"Oh, and no sweats, jeans, slacks or T-shirts. I want to see some leg, so put on one of those dresses stashed in the back of your closet."

She whipped her head around. "A *dress*? Bryse, come on,"

she whined. "Can't I just put on a pair of slacks with a nice blouse?"

Bryson smiled. "Nope. This is a real date. Dinner at a fancy restaurant, wine, candles, you know that kind of stuff." He tweaked her nose. "And stop pouting," he added with a chuckle.

Raven turned back to the water. "The last time I dressed up, it took longer to get ready than the actual date lasted."

He instinctively knew she was talking about her last date. "You don't have to worry about our date ending like the other one. I promise I'll make it worth your time."

"All right. But only because I like you."

Bryson threw his head back and laughed. "We'll go with that then. For the record, I like you, too." He came to his feet and extended his hand.

Raven grasped his hand and he pulled her to her feet. She leaned up and kissed his cheek. "Thanks, Bryse."

"For what?"

"For giving me time to get used to us. You asked me what you could do to help me and I said nothing. But you're doing it just by being you." She laid her head on his chest. "Please don't ever change."

His heart full, he whispered, "I won't." He promised himself from this moment on that he would do everything in his power to make her happy and that she would never regret taking a chance on him.

* * *

Raven dried off, smoothed lotion on and put on her bra and panties. She walked out of the bathroom and went into her closet to search for a dress. "And how did he know they were stuffed in the back?" she muttered while pulling out one after the other. The only reason she had so many was because Erika had dragged her shopping on more than one occasion, citing that Raven needed something to wear just in case she had a hot date. Her hand landed on the eggplant-colored dress she'd worn on her date with Darren and she immediately shoved it back in its place. She frowned. Just the memory of what happened tempted her to torch it. Maybe she'd donate it because she couldn't ever see herself wearing it again. The sound of her doorbell interrupted her mental tirade. Raven peeked over at the clock. It was only five thirty. What was Bryson doing here so early? She started to put on her robe, but changed her mind. Just because they'd slept together didn't mean she would start answering the door half dressed. She quickly pulled on a pair of shorts and a tee and rushed to the door.

She stood stunned at the sight of her brother leaning against the wall. "Simeon! What are you doing here? I thought you weren't coming back until next week sometime."

Simeon lifted a brow. "Hello to you too, sis. Are you going to let me in or keep me standing out here like a solicitor?"

Raven backed up and let him in.

He kissed her cheek and walked into the living room. "How are you?"

"Good. You still didn't answer my question."

He made himself comfortable in one of the chairs anchoring her sofa. "The date on one of my cases changed and I have to get back to work on Monday to prepare."

"How're Mom and Dad?" she asked, taking the other chair.

"They're doing well. Mom said she'll call you next week. Dad's talking about him and Mom going on one of those month-long cruises."

"Are you serious? That's great. They've been talking about taking one for a long time." She glanced over at the clock to see how much time she had before needing to get dressed.

Simeon chuckled. "Yeah. I guess now that Dad has expanded his medical practice, he feels more comfortable leaving."

"Good for him." Their dad had been the town's physician since before she was born. "I know you saw the whole town."

"Just about." He rattled off the names of relatives and friends they knew. "Ava told me to tell you hello. She and Owen seem to be doing well. Then of course, the question came up about my status." He groaned, slid down in the chair and covered his eyes. "You would not believe the number of people who asked me whether I'm dating someone seriously, engaged or married. And Mom was the worst."

Raven laughed. When she'd gone home for Ava's wedding, her mother had made a point of reminding her that Raven and Ava were the same age and asked when she could expect to have the same mother-of-the-bride privilege. Raven had circumvented the question the entire week, especially since she had broken up with her boyfriend a few weeks before after seeing him kissing another woman. She glanced over at the clock again.

"She told me about every person around our age who's gotten married in the last year, who had babies and who was expecting. In a way, I was glad to cut the visit short." Simeon yawned and stretched.

"You look tired. Maybe you should go home and take a nap." Raven wanted him to be gone before Bryson arrived. Even though they knew each other, Simeon would be suspicious if she came out wearing a dress, knowing how much she hated wearing them.

"I am a little tired." He stood.

*Thank goodness!* Her relief was short-lived as he kicked off his shoes and stretched his six-foot frame across her sofa. Now what? She checked the time again. Bryson would be there in less than an hour and she needed to change. It wouldn't be a problem if she didn't have to get all dressed up.

"Do you have somewhere to be or something? That's like the fourth or fifth time you've looked at the clock."

Raven didn't realize he'd seen her. "Just hanging out with an old friend for a while," she said nonchalantly, hoping he'd take the hint and leave. "I was about to change when you got here."

Simeon eyed her a long moment. "Don't mind me. Go ahead and get dressed."

That was not what she wanted to hear, but she didn't have a choice. She stalked to her bedroom, grumbling about nosy, annoying little brothers. She knew he only wanted to stay to find out who she was spending her time with. She took a deep breath. "Relax, Raven. He knows Bryson and I have been friends for forever and go out all the time," she repeated under her breath. She took down the black dress that Erika had bought six months ago and still had the tag attached. It stopped mid-thigh, had a halter neckline and, aside from a four-inch wide strip of fabric with cutouts down the center, left her upper back bare. Raven thought the dress a little too risqué for her tastes. It had caused a minor argument in the store and, when Raven refused to purchase it, Erika did. As they left the store, her cousin shoved the bag at her and told her she expected her to wear it with authority. Sighing, she took it off the hanger and slipped it on. Raven walked over to the full-length mirror in the bathroom. Bryson said he wanted to see some leg. Wearing this, he'd see more than enough. She applied her makeup, buckled her four-inch black sandals that had one thin strap across the toe and one around her ankle and took a deep breath. She grabbed the small matching black purse and wrap then headed back to the living room.

Simeon bolted upright on the sofa. "*Damn,* sis! Is that you?" Then a scowl covered his handsome face. "Old friend, my ass. Who is he?"

Raven laughed. "Just Bryson, so you can stand down on your big, bad brother routine."

"I don't ever recall you dressing like this to hang out with Bryson."

"That's because I don't tell you every time we hang out." And because she'd never dressed like this for anyone. Ever. "Now that you know who it is, you can leave."

"Nah, I think I'll stick around for this. I haven't seen Bryse in a while. Are y'all meeting Jerome and Kendrick, too?"

She tried to keep the irritation off her face. "No."

He stroked his goatee. "This is getting more interesting by the moment."

"Don't you have a flavor-of-the-month you need to call?"

"I don't have a flavor-of-the-month. I'm happily single these days because most women have a problem with the long hours I have to put in at the firm." Being three years out of law school, he worked hard to make a name for himself. "Since when did the two of you start hanging out *alone*?"

"Since twelve years ago. And we all just were out last night. I've done the same thing with Ken and Rome, so it's no big deal. Go home, Simeon. This is not a courtroom and I'm not on the witness stand."

A slow grin made its way across Simeon's mouth. "I think you're not telling me something."

Raven placed her hands on her hips. "You're correct. I'm not telling you anything." The doorbell rang. He made a move to stand and she leveled him with a glare that froze him in place. "This is not your house and you don't open my door unless I ask you to." She pivoted and went to let Bryson in. She stifled a moan when she saw him standing there wearing a charcoal gray suit that she knew had been tailored just for him. With his towering height, clean-shaven face and those sexy locs flowing over his shoulders, he was every woman's fantasy come true. Raven finally found her voice. "Hey, Bryse."

He didn't move or utter a word.

"Bryse?"

"You look good, girl."

"Thanks. Come in. My brother's here."

"Yeah, I know. I recognized his car." Simeon's cobalt blue mustang was hard to miss.

She turned and started back to the living room and heard Bryse curse. "What?"

Bryse said for her ears only, "You'd better be glad your brother is here."

Raven read the meaning in his eyes, loud and clear.

"Hey, Simeon," Bryson said.

"What's up, Bryson." They did a one-arm hug. "It's been a

minute. How're things at the center?"

"Going well. I'm sure Raven will fill you in on what we've got coming up. How's life in the courtroom?"

"Busy. That's why I had to come back early from my vacation."

"I know how that goes." Bryson turned his attention to Raven. "You ready?"

"Yep." She glared at her brother.

Simeon chuckled, put on his shoes and pushed to his feet. "I can take a hint."

Raven snorted. "If you could take a hint, you'd be already gone."

He looked affronted. "See how she treats me, man?"

Bryson laughed.

Simeon planted a kiss on Raven's temple and whispered, "We're definitely going to talk about this." He preceded them out of the door.

Raven locked up and walked to Bryson's car. Out of the corner of her eye, she saw her brother observing them curiously, but she didn't look his way. He backed out of the space and she threw up a wave as he passed.

Bryson opened the door and waited for her to get in. Instead of closing it, he popped the trunk of his Audi by remote, came back with a dozen red roses and handed them to her. "I had planned to give them to you at the door, but I saw Simeon's car and didn't know if you wanted him to know, so I waited."

"They're beautiful, Bryse, and thank you." He smiled and closed the door. He was making it difficult to keep from falling for him. The fragrant flowers filled the car's interior.

He got in on his side and started the car, but didn't immediately pull off. His gaze swept over her with naked desire. "Raven, you look absolutely stunning. You make me want to cancel the plans I made and keep you home. I hope I don't have to act a fool tonight."

Raven's mouth dropped. "What does that mean?"

"If a man so much as glances your way, there are going to be problems."

She smiled. "Just drive." In the past when they'd gone out, he had displayed a level of possessiveness that reminded her of her brother. However, this time his tone and look indicated something else entirely. She didn't bother to ask where they were going, just made herself comfortable and observed the passing scenery. Forty minutes later, he pulled up to the valet in front of Lawry's The Prime Rib restaurant in Beverly Hills.

Bryson turned the car over to the valet, escorted Raven in and gave his name to the hostess. They were seated in a booth and had their drink orders taken within five minutes.

"This is nice. I like your style, Mr. Montgomery." The booths lined the walls, tables for four were arranged in the middle of the floor, and expensive chandeliers hung from the ceiling.

"Thanks."

They spent a few minutes poring over the menu and both decided on the signature prime rib. The server came back with their glasses of champagne and took their dinner order.

Bryson raised his glass. "To the beginning of something beautiful."

Raven touched her glass to his, their eyes never leaving each other while they sipped.

"So, tell me about this marriage pact you mentioned. We never got around to finishing the conversation that night."

Her face warmed with the remembrance. After all the screaming she'd done, it was a wonder none of her neighbors had come banging on the door. She took another gulp of her champagne. "It was something we did to get Quinn off our backs. She's into romance and after Ava's wedding, she was feeling all mushy and talked us into agreeing that we'd be married within a year."

"You said Mac and Ryleigh have already gotten married."

"Yeah, which surprised the heck out of us because neither

of them had ever relationships that lasted past the moment. At least we were there for Mac's wedding. Ryleigh eloped."

"Hmm, interesting. Ava got married in September, which means you have roughly three months to make good on the pact."

"Something like that," Raven murmured. She had no chance of making that deadline and the feeling left her strangely disheartened. "So do you guys have everything in place for the summer program?" she asked, changing the subject.

Bryson smiled knowingly, but to his credit didn't push. "Just about. We'll have the new laptops on Tuesday and meet with the teachers we hired on Wednesday." He paused when the server returned with their salads, which they prepared tableside in a spinning stainless-steel bowl atop a larger one filled with ice. He thanked the man. "I mentioned your idea to Tonya," he continued, "and you should've seen her. She said she would start working on a program proposal for me."

"Very cool." That he'd taken her suggestion spoke volumes about his confidence in her and she sensed the wall around her heart cracking. He continued to share his vision while they ate and she was even more impressed. When they were done, he talked her into sharing dessert. They opted for the warm apple pie topped with vanilla ice cream. The food had been excellently prepared, the service outstanding and the company exceptional. Hands down, it was the best date she'd ever had.

Bryson settled the bill, helped her with the wrap and escorted her out to wait for the car.

After they were in the car, Raven placed a hand on Bryson's arm. "I really enjoyed myself. Thank you."

"You're welcome. The night's not over yet."

She studied him. "I thought we were just going to dinner."

He grinned. "I never said that." He leaned over, kissed her and drove off.

The next stop turned out to be a dance club that played funk, hip-hop and R&B music. She had a ball even though her feet complained about being in heels for such a long time. They danced to song after song. She did a little spin move that had her swaying with her back to Bryson, her arms in the air. He came up behind her, placed his hands on her waist and moved with her for a moment before stepping back. She rotated until she faced him again. Bryson stopped dancing and slowly came toward her. The look in his eyes made her breath catch. Everything faded away—the noise, the music—except the man in front of her. He bent and captured her mouth in a long, drugging kiss that turned her knees to jelly and sent a sweet ache flowing through every part of her body. She clung to him as he devoured her mouth in the middle of the dance floor.

Bryson lifted his head. "Let's get out of here."

Still reeling, she let him lead her out of the club and into the car. She sat with her eyes closed, waiting for her heart rate to return to normal. The sexual tension was so high that if either of them spoke they'd be on the side of the road and naked in a flash. She felt the car going around curves and opened her eyes. He was driving through a neighborhood in the hills and came to a stop at an open area that overlooked the city.

"Do you want to get out for a minute?"

"Yes." When they got out, he placed his jacket around her shoulders and the faint notes of his cologne drifted up to her nose and she resisted the urge to bury her face in the warm, earthy fragrance. The black velvet sky was filled with stars and they had a clear view of the city below.

Bryson turned her to face him and tilted her chin. "You take my breath away with your beauty, inside and out. You are mine, Raven Holloway."

Before she could fully process his statement, she was, once again, swept away by his kiss. And she decided that yes, for tonight, she would be his.

# Chapter Seven

Sunday morning, the ringing phone startled Raven awake. She blindly searched for it on the nightstand. "Hello," she mumbled. She'd had a restless night dreaming about Bryson and the impact of his words.

"Hey, girl," a chorus of voices said, sounding way too chipper for the hour—Mackenzie, Ryleigh and Quinn.

She opened one eye, squinted at the clock and groaned. "It is eight thirty in the frigging morning. Why are you all calling me at this hour? Somebody better be dying."

Quinn giggled. "Oh yeah, we forgot it's three hours earlier in LA."

"Yeah, three hours *earlier*."

"Aw, we're sorry."

Raven flipped over on her back. "Mac, lightning is going to strike you dead lying like that." More laughter came through the line. "So, why are y'all calling me at the crack of dawn?" Like she didn't already know. Since Mac and Ryleigh had gotten married, every month they called to get an update on Raven and Quinn to see if they were any closer to following them down the aisle.

"How's Darren?" Ryleigh asked.

"I have no idea."

"Um, what does that mean?"

"Exactly what I said. One minute he was talking about us moving toward something more permanent, the next, after a couple of my clients stopped by the table, he decided that he couldn't handle me working with athletes and suggested I get a job more to his liking so he wouldn't have to worry about them flirting with me. Then he had the nerve to grab my arm."

"I would've punched him in the throat," Ryleigh said.

"I wanted to, but we were out to dinner. I just agreed that we were moving toward something permanent—him being permanently out of my life."

"Oh, Raven, I'm so sorry."

"It's no big deal, Quinn."

"Yes, it is. I was hoping you were going to tell us that you were either engaged or close to it."

Mac chimed in, "Girl, don't worry. Some other guy is going to show up. Mark my words."

Raven didn't have to mark her words. Another guy did show up, one that had been in front of her face the whole time.

"Yeah, girl," Ryleigh said. "Do you need us to come down? You know we'll be right there."

"I'm fine."

"You sure? Because we can scout out a few new prospects."

"No thanks, Ryleigh. I don't need a new prospect. I already have one. Well, he's not new and he's not really a prospect. Well…I mean…"

"Raven. Just tell us who it is."

"It's Bryson." They were silent for a full minute then their screams came through the line. She jerked the phone away from her ear.

"It's about damn time," Ryleigh said.

"Right," Mac agreed. "I would've jumped his fine ass a long time ago.

"Friends to lovers. That's so romantic."

Of course, that would be the first thing out of Quinn's mouth.

"I just want to know how he is in bed? Can he bring it or

what?"

"Mac, why is that always the first question with you?" Mac had been the queen of one-night stands until the last one backfired and she ended up married.

"Come on, Raven, you know that's a requirement for any candidate. No sense in wasting your time on a man who can't even make you wet."

"Girl, that's the truth," Ryleigh said.

Raven sighed. She loved her girls, but sometimes they got out of control. "The answer is yes. It was all that and more." She recalled every moment of that evening from the first unsure kiss and wonder of the moment to the featherlike caresses of his hands and mouth and the feel of him thrusting deep inside, setting her body on fire and making her scream his name over and over.

"Raven!" Mac, Quinn and Ryleigh chorused.

"What?"

"Evidently, Bryson did more than bring it if the mere mention sends you off into fantasy land," Mac teased.

Quinn squealed. "Ooh, so are you two dating now or was it a one night thing that kind of just happened?"

"We're sort of dating. He wants us to see where this goes."

"You don't sound so sure about it, though."

"Don't get me wrong, Ryleigh, Bryson is a great guy, one of the best, but it is freaking me out because we've been friends for twelve years and not *once* did I ever think of him as anything other than a friend." She shared the details of how he had comforted her about the breakup with Darren. "It was just like always at first, then something changed. He touched me and I felt…I don't know. *Something*. He felt it, too. Then he kissed me and the next thing I knew, I didn't want him to stop and we were in my bed. But I don't want to lose my best friend if this doesn't work out."

Mac's sigh came through the line. "Please don't tell me you're trying to friend zone that brother."

"Well, not exactly, but I don't want to get too close, just in case. He's making it really hard, though."

"If he wants to be with you, he's supposed to make it hard for you to resist." Raven heard papers rustling then Quinn came back on the line. "I was reading an article about how you can tell if a man is really into you."

They all groaned.

"No, listen. It's says he'll make time for you, even if he's busy, call you or text you just to say hello. Ooh, and here's the good part. During sex he'll make eye contact with you or kiss you on the forehead, and after sex, he'll want to cuddle with you, instead of leaving right away. There's some other stuff about humor, having a career versus a job and a rate-your-mate scale. I can send you the article and you can see how Bryson measures up."

Raven didn't need to fill out any scale to know how Bryson would measure up. He'd rate at the top of the list in every area. "No, thanks. I don't need it."

"That's because Bryson did everything I read, huh?"

"No comment."

The women screamed with laughter and Ryleigh started humming the Wedding March.

"Just don't do like Ryleigh and sneak off and get married. We want to be there," Mac said.

"Y'all know I don't like a lot of hoopla," Ryleigh mumbled.

"Who said anything about getting married? I'm just trying to get used to the fact that I slept with my best friend."

"In a way, that's a good thing, Raven," Quinn said. "He already knows the things that make you happy."

"I guess." If last night was any indication, he could be elected president of the Make Raven Happy fan club. "Last night, he took me out to dinner at Lawry's, then dancing. Afterward, we ended up in the hills overlooking the city." She ran her hand over her face. Why did she just tell them that?

"Hot damn! Bryson is *the man*."

"My thoughts exactly, Ryleigh. Girl, I'm sending you a

high-five."

"Got it, Mac."

"Are you two finished?" Ryleigh and Mac had always been the wild ones, and Mac had a thing about being first in everything.

"I totally get what you're saying about this transition from friends to lovers, Raven. But it sounds like he's still the same Bryson, only now things are a little more intimate. We know all about what you say is your track record with men. Don't let your fears stop you from being happy because I believe he could be the one for you."

Quinn had always been the voice of reason when it came to romance, even though she drove them crazy with all of her articles and quizzes on love. "Thanks, Quinn."

"At least the three of you will make the deadline."

"Quinn, if you put away all those lists and articles and just be yourself, you'll be right with us," Mac said. "So, what are you going to do, Raven?"

"The only thing I can. And pray I don't end up with another broken heart." *Or worse, lose my best friend.*

* * *

Thursday evening, Bryson stood under the frigid spray, hoping to calm his body. Five days. It had been five days since he left Raven at her door and he'd been in a constant state of arousal from that moment until now. And no amount of cold showers, thoughts of baseball or blizzards had helped. The only thing that would douse the raging fire threatening to consume him was making love with Raven. It had taken every ounce of his control Saturday night to walk away. He'd read the desire in her eyes, the expectation of what should follow, then the question when it didn't.

It would be easy for them to jump into bed every time because the chemistry between them was strong, but he wanted this relationship to be different than his previous ones.

Bryson turned the water to warm and washed up. He heard

the doorbell just as he finished drying off. Rushing out of the bathroom, he pulled on a pair of basketball shorts and grabbed a T-shirt out of the drawer, putting it on as he walked to the door. He flipped on the porch light and checked the peephole. *Raven?* What was she doing here at this hour? Bryson snatched the door open. "Hey, Raven." He pulled her into the house and closed the door. "Is everything okay?" Her hair had been pulled up into a ragged ponytail, she had on a pair of shorts and a tee, and flip flops. He searched her face. She'd never come over to his house late at night unannounced.

"Yeah. Can we talk?"

"Of course. Come on in. Can I get you something to drink?" He guided her to the family room and gestured for her to sit.

"No, I'm fine." She perched on the edge of the sofa.

Bryson waited for her to speak. When she didn't say anything for a couple of minutes, he scooted closer to her. "What is it that you want to talk about, sweetheart?" he prompted gently.

"I…" Raven seemed to struggle with her words.

"We've never had a problem talking to each other and now is no different."

She squared her shoulders and shifted to face him. "You're right. I think I want you to kiss me."

The corner of his mouth kicked up into a lazy smile and he lifted a brow. "You think? As in you're not sure."

She stared at him. Her gaze dropped to his mouth briefly, then moved back up to his face. "Yes, I'm sure. I want you to kiss me."

"Good, because I'm very sure I want to kiss you." Bryson crushed his mouth to hers. The kiss was hot and demanding, but filled with a sweetness that flooded his soul. For a long while, he fed himself on her kisses—some soft and gentle, others sensual and intense. But all left him mindlessly intoxicated with the taste and uniqueness that was Raven. Her breathless sighs and small whimpers of pleasure had him as hard as he'd ever been. Feeling himself hovering on the brink of losing control, he eased back.

"Where did you learn to kiss like this?" Raven murmured, kissing him again.

He took over the kiss, deepened it, twining his tongue with hers. "The way I kiss depends on the woman I'm kissing and your kisses," he said, still nibbling on her lips, "are sweeter than the most expensive chocolate. They fuel my passion. *You* fuel my passion." Unable to help himself, Bryson captured her mouth again, absorbing her essence into his very cells.

"We need to take this to your bedroom."

His straining erection throbbed in agreement. "Not tonight, baby. As much as I'd like to, you and I both have to work in the morning."

Raven groaned in protest. She lifted her arm and checked her watch. "It's only eleven forty-five."

He chuckled. "Ah, I think your watch stopped." He gestured to the clock on the wall.

Her eyes widened. "It's after one in the morning. We've been kissing for *two hours*?"

"Hey. When it's good…" He shrugged.

"And you are *very* good," she said sultrily, reaching down to stroke him.

Bryson jerked upright. He grabbed her hand and placed a kiss on the back. "Stop that." He set her away from him, closed his eyes and drew in several deep breaths. He had never been so tempted by a woman in his life. "I'm going to get my shoes, keys and wallet so I can follow you home."

"You don't need to do that. I'll just text you when I get there."

He shook his head. "No deal. I have never let you go home alone at this hour and I'm not about to start." Over the years, he, Kendrick and Jerome alternated following her home whenever they were out together past a certain time. But now that she belonged to him, he planned to take sole responsibility for her safety and wellbeing. "Be right back."

Bryson stuck his feet into his slides, and grabbed his wallet and keys from the dresser. Any other time he would take full advantage of what they both obviously craved, but he needed to prove to her that they were more than just bed buddies. He could get that from any woman. What he wanted from Raven was a commitment. He wanted her heart, with no reservations. He, who had gone more than a decade shying away from commitment, now wanted exactly that. And he had promised not to rush things. Bryson saw another cold shower in his immediate future. *It's going to be a long night.*

# Chapter Eight

Friday morning, Raven was still thinking about last night with Bryson. She had never known a man's kisses could stir her emotions to the level they had. The other men in her past had used kissing as a means to an end, at no time going past a minute or two before wanting to jump into bed. However, Bryson treated kissing as if it were an act unto itself. She couldn't believe that they had spent two hours kissing. No sex. Just spine-tingling, toe-curling, slow-as-molasses kisses. She knew he wanted more—the huge bulge in his shorts said so—and, truthfully, so had she. If he had even hinted at wanting to go further, she would have been all over him. But that he held back out of concern for her being tired at work only endeared him to her more.

*The way I kiss depends on the woman I'm kissing and your kisses are sweeter than the most expensive chocolate. They fuel my passion. You fuel my passion.* His words came back to her in a heated rush, sending a shiver down her spine. All of his kisses had been amazing, but the one that followed those words had been different, connecting them on a deeper level that shocked and terrified her. Even so, against her better judgment, the cracks in her walls widened and she felt herself falling harder for him.

David poked his head in the office. "Hey, Raven. Chris is here."

"I'll be right there." Raven looked at the computer screen and realized she hadn't entered one thing. "I have got to stop thinking about him," she muttered and closed the file.

"Hey. There she is." A smile lit Chris's handsome dark face.

She shook her head. "Hey, Chris. How's the back today?"

"Not bad. I think my flexibility is getting better." He laid down on the mat and started doing his stretches. "I think I can handle a couple more strengthening exercises."

"We'll see."

"You think I'll be ready for next season?"

"Only your doctor can answer that, but I'll do everything I can to help."

While going through his strengthening routine, Chris said, "I'm glad you got rid of the dude we met at the restaurant." He made a face. "He was way too uptight and not your type."

Raven folded her arms. "Who said I got rid of him and how do you know my type?"

"Come on, girl. His face was all pinched when we were introduced. He couldn't even take a joke and looked like he'd been sucking on lemons. He acted like Bernard and I were going to run off with you."

"You got all that from a one-minute introduction?" He was dead on, but she had no intention of saying so.

"Absolutely. And he wasn't looking at you right."

She let out a short bark of laughter. "What?"

"Anybody who saw you together would think it was all business." Chris sat up. Now, the brother you had dinner with at Lawry's on Saturday...*that's* how you're supposed to look at your woman."

Her mouth fell open. "So, you're following me around on weekends now?"

He laughed. "Not on purpose. Hey, don't I get credit for not interrupting, though?"

Raven thought about the differences between Bryson and Darren. Bryson wouldn't have cared one bit about Chris coming to the table to speak because he was confident enough to know that Raven wouldn't flirt with or see another man while they were together. "You're supposed to be counting."

"I know this routine by heart. I don't have to count. You dating the new guy?"

"Why are you in my business, Chris? I don't get in yours."

"That's because everything I do is already out in the public." He lowered his voice. "But I do have a new lady and I think she might be the one."

"Congratulations."

He slowly came to his feet. "Thanks. And congratulations to you, too." He sauntered off to the leg press.

Raven stood there in disbelief for a second, and then shook herself. Chris had seen too much. Thank goodness her life wasn't under a microscope like his. If she felt uncomfortable with Chris asking her questions about Bryson, she couldn't imagine what it would be like for him with the media constantly in his business.

On his way out later, Chris said, "I know I was messing with you earlier, but I am serious about the new guy. You looked happy and so did he. But then again, I'd be happy too seeing you in that dress."

She couldn't help smiling at his crazy humor. "Bye, Chris. And try not to follow me this weekend."

He tossed her a bold wink and a megawatt smile then strolled out.

She went back to the office to finish the charting from the morning before eating lunch. One of the receptionists had gone out for food and brought Raven a chicken salad back and Raven took it down to the break room to eat. There were a couple other people eating and reading. She chose a table to herself, not really feeling like making small talk.

Raven had finally remembered to bring her earphones today and put them in, selected a playlist and opened her salad. While eating she checked her emails and messages. Her brother had sent a message saying they needed to talk. She rolled her eyes and didn't respond. The next one was from Bryson. She read: *Hey, beautiful. Just checking to see how your day is going and to let you know I'm thinking about you. See you tonight.*

She put her fork down. How was she supposed to resist this man? Her thumb hovered over the *reply* button and before she could chicken out, she hit it and typed back: *Thinking about you, too.* And she had been. All. Day. Long. Bryson did make her happy and she was going to do her best to hold on to that happiness for as long as it lasted.

They were supposed to hang out with Jerome and Kendrick tonight and Bryson had insisted on picking her up this time. Though neither man had said anything last time, Raven had been able to cover up her feelings for Bryson. She didn't think it would happen tonight.

* * *

Late Friday, Bryson and Jerome loaded the last program on the new laptops and locked them in the cabinet.

"I have one more thing to do, then I'll be ready to head over to the restaurant," Jerome said.

"I'll meet you guys there. I'm going to pick up Raven first."

"Aw, that's so sweet."

"Go to hell, Rome." Bryson strode out of the room with Jerome's laughter following. In his office, he packed up his laptop and folders containing information he wanted to review over the weekend and locked the door. "I'm gone," he called out as he passed Jerome's office. Tonya had already left for the day. On the way home he called Raven.

"Hey, Bryse."

"Hey. I should probably make it to your house around six thirty. I'm going home to change first."

"That's fine. It'll give me time to change, too."

"You wouldn't happen to have another one of those dresses like the one you had on Saturday, would you?"

"Even if I did, I wouldn't wear it."

Bryson laughed. "Just thought I'd ask."

"Bye." Raven hung up.

He didn't mind her not wearing a dress because he planned to see much more than her legs tonight.

Because of traffic, he was ten minutes later than the time he'd told Raven. Instead of parking in a space, he pulled up behind her car, left the car running and knocked on her door.

Raven opened the door and stepped out. "I'm ready."

His jaw went slack. His gaze made a slow tour down her body and back up. She had on a dark blue halter dress that hugged every curve and stopped mid-thigh, with a pair of low-heeled sandals. "You are trying to kill me." She smiled and walked past him with a switch in her hips he'd never seen.

"Don't say I've never done anything for you."

Bryson caught up with her and opened the car door. When she got in, her dress inched up higher and an involuntary groan slipped from his throat. As he went around to his side, he wondered how mad Jerome and Kendrick would be if he and Raven didn't show up. Pushing the thought aside, he got in, let his gaze roam over her once more and drove off. That extended kissing session last night had taken his arousal to a level that he'd never experienced, but he had plans for them tonight. "I never knew you were such a tease."

She gave him a sidelong glance. "I'm not. But being with you has me doing things I wouldn't typically do."

Her words made him smile. "Is that good or bad?"

"I don't know. What do you think?"

"As your best friend, I think you can be and do anything you want and only you can decide what that will be. As a man who is falling for you by the minute, I think it's very good." He reached for her hand. "You are a beautiful and sexy woman, Raven, and it's okay to let that part of you out sometimes. You've never done this with any of your other boyfriends?"

"No." She paused for a moment. "They never seemed interested. Aside from the last two jerks, the others were more enamored by where I worked and what they thought I could give them, like tickets to sports games."

No wonder she was so reluctant to start up with him. He'd probably be the same way if all the women he had dated treated him that way. "Well, you won't have to worry about that with me."

"I never have," she said softly, turning toward the window.

They completed the rest of the drive in companionable silence. Bryson spotted Jerome and Kendrick as soon as he stepped through the door of the restaurant. "I need to warn you about something," he said to Raven.

Raven glanced up at him with concern. "What?"

"I will be holding your hand, touching you, putting my arm around you, and maybe even sneaking in a kiss or two while we're here. So, get ready."

She rolled her eyes. "I thought something happened."

"Something did." He entwined their fingers and started toward the guys, humming You Put A Move On My Heart by Tamia. When they reached the table, Bryson said, "Sorry we're late. Traffic." Their eyes were riveted to Raven.

"Damn," Jerome whispered in awe. "Raven, girl, you look amazing."

"Thanks. Ken, stop staring like you've never seen a woman in a dress."

Kendrick finally found his voice. "Uh…sorry. It's just that you never… *Wow!*"

She reached up and closed his mouth. "Sit down. It's just a dress. I don't act all crazy when you put on a suit."

Bryson and Jerome laughed.

Kendrick kissed her cheek. "You're right. But you're still cute. You clean up well, girl."

Bryson pulled out Raven's chair then took the one next to her. "Did you guys order yet?"

"No. They seated us a minute before you got here." Jerome passed them menus. By the time the server came, they were ready to place both their food and drink orders. They made small talk for a few minutes and Bryson and Jerome caught Kendrick up on information he'd missed for the summer program. The conversation stopped when the server came back with their drinks. They thanked the woman and she departed with a smile.

"I'll be ready to start next week," Kendrick said, picking up where they left off. He leaned forward and clasped his hands on the table. "So, what's up with you two?"

Bryson and Raven shared a look. Bryson said, "We're dating."

Jerome lifted his glass in mock salute. "I'm happy for you guys." He turned to Raven. "He's lucky I'm letting him have a chance with you first. But if he acts up, I got you."

Raven laughed. "I'll keep that in mind."

"Maybe you should've made your move before now," Bryson said without cracking a smile, "because she won't ever be available again." They all went silent.

Raven choked on her tea.

"Well, damn," Kendrick said.

Jerome shook his head in wonder. "Ditto."

Bryson took a long swig of his beer. He hadn't meant to say those words just yet, and definitely not without saying them to Raven first. But the moment they left his mouth, in his heart, he knew they were true. He was in this for the long haul and intended to show Raven just what that entailed.

Jerome raised his glass. "To Bryson and Raven. I get to be the best man at the wedding."

Bryson hazarded a glance Raven's way. She appeared to still be in shock. He placed his arm around her and gave her shoulders a gentle squeeze. "Everything is okay, sweetheart," he whispered against her ear and kissed her temple. Bryson and Raven endured more teasing over dinner. Raven finally relaxed and reverted back to her old self. When it came time to leave, Kendrick and Jerome hugged Raven and warned Bryson to take good care of her.

Bryson waved them off. "Yeah, yeah. Go home. I'll see you guys on Monday." Once in the car, he asked Raven, "Are you okay?"

She nodded. "Yep."

Though she said she was okay, Raven sat quietly during the drive. He sincerely hoped he hadn't messed up.

"We're going to your house?" Raven asked when he pulled into his garage.

"I thought we could spend some quiet time together, if that's okay. We can go somewhere else, if you like."

"Yes, it's okay. And here is fine."

He smiled and caressed her cheek.

As soon as they got into the house, she removed her shoes and dropped down on the sofa. "If I had known we were coming back here, I would've brought a change of clothes. I don't want to have to wear this dress all night."

It was on the tip of his tongue to tell her she wouldn't have the dress on long. If he got his way, she'd be out of it in the next ten minutes. "You want something?"

"No way. I'm full. Those crab cakes were really good." She patted the space next to her.

Bryson sat and draped his arm around her.

"What did you mean tonight?"

He released a deep breath. "Exactly what I said. I'm in this for the duration, Raven. And before you say anything, I had planned to say it to you first, but not so soon, because I didn't want to overwhelm you. You're still adjusting to us and, although this thing with us seems to be moving at the speed of light, my feelings are true."

"Thank you for being honest with me, Bryse."

"Always, sweetheart."

"You're right. It does scare me, but I can't stop what I'm beginning to feel for you."

"Then we're going down this road together. You don't have to be afraid. All you have to do is embrace what I want to give you."

Raven sat up. "And what is that?"

Holding her gaze, he said, "Me. I want to give you me." Bryson covered his mouth with hers and let his kiss communicate everything he wanted to say.

She broke off the kiss. "Bryson," she whispered.

He stood, swept her up in his arms and carried her upstairs to his bedroom. He placed her on her feet, turned her around, released the clasp on her dress and slid the zipper down. He squatted so she could step out and laid it carefully on the back of a chair. The lamp on his nightstand provided enough light for him to see the alluring picture she made standing in the middle of his room wearing nothing but a black lace bra and matching bikini panties. Bryson stroked a finger along the top of her breasts visible above the bra. "I like this." He dropped his head and replaced his finger with his tongue. He moved back to her mouth.

Raven unbuttoned his shirt and pushed it off his shoulders. "I like this, too."

She trailed her tongue over his chest and abdomen, the heat of her mouth scorching him from the inside out. He finished undressing them and donned a condom. He took a moment to turn the covers back and kissed her down onto the bed. He left her mouth and placed soft, butterfly kisses along her jaw, throat and her breasts. He circled his tongue around the nipple before pulling it into his mouth. Bryson shifted his body, used his knee to spread her legs and pushed at her entrance. "Look at me, Raven."

She moaned and lifted her eyes to his.

"This is not sex. I'm making love to my woman." Not taking his eyes off her, he slid into her warmth until he was sheathed completely. He withdrew and thrust deeply, setting a sensual rhythm that made them both shudder. He ground his body into hers, gyrating in slow, insistent circles.

Raven clung to him, whispering his name over and over. "Don't stop."

"I don't plan to." Covering her mouth with his own, he moved his tongue in and out of her mouth, imitating the movements of his lower body.

She arched up to meet his measured strokes, while her hands moved up and down his back. Her cries of pleasure filled the room. "*Yesssssss!*"

"That's right. Give yourself to me," Bryson murmured, keeping up the unhurried pace. He felt her body start to tremble around him and lifted her higher, stroking her harder, wanting to be as deep as possible when she came. Raven let out a scream that sent chills down his spine. He pulled out to the tip and surged back in. His orgasm exploded through him with a force that rocked his soul. He buried his head in the hollow of her neck. "Raven, you're mine, baby." And at that moment he knew he was in love with his best friend.

# Chapter Nine

Raven woke up Saturday morning in bed next to Bryson, thinking about what he'd told her about being in the relationship for the long haul. She wanted to believe in them because, even though it had been less than a month, she had fallen in love with him. But would it last? She carefully shifted and watched him sleep. She couldn't think of a time since she had known him that he hadn't been there for her. Raven fell back against the pillow and closed her eyes. Why was this so hard? *Because you don't want your heart to get broken again,* an inner voice chimed.

"I'm not sure how I feel about waking up and seeing a frown on your face after such a beautiful night. Was it that bad?"

She couldn't hide her smile. She punched him playfully on the shoulder. "You know it wasn't." He'd given her more orgasms in one night than she'd had with all the other guys she'd been with, combined. She'd lost count after that third round.

"Then what's on your mind?"

"Just thinking about everything you said last night."

Bryson propped himself up on his elbow. "And?"

Quinn's words rang in her ears. *Don't let your fears stop you from being happy because I believe he could be the one for you.* "And I'm in this for the duration, too."

"I love you, Raven."

She gasped.

"I know you're not there yet and we'll still go as slow as you need, but whenever you get here, I'll be waiting."

If she didn't love him already, that would have pushed her over the edge. "I'm there, Bryse. I want to embrace all that you're offering. I want you." He looked at her with such tenderness and love it brought tears to her eyes.

He wrapped his arms around her and held her close to his heart. "You have me, baby."

Raven closed her eyes and smiled, feeling a sense of contentment she had never experienced. Her stomach growled. She heard the deep rumble of Bryson's laughter against her ear.

"Somebody needs to eat. I'll fix us some breakfast."

"I don't have anything to wear or a toothbrush."

"I washed your bra and panties while you were asleep and there's a new travel kit in the bathroom."

She eyed him.

"Yep, I planned for you to spend the night." Bryson sat up. "Do you want to go first? Or we could shower together."

"You can go first," she said quickly.

Chuckling, he flipped the covers back and went into the bathroom.

She watched him until he disappeared around the corner. A smile curved her lips. Mac was right. Raven should have jumped his sexy ass a long time ago.

When it was her turn, he set out towels and pointed out the travel kit.

"We could have saved time if we'd showered together," he said.

The granite shower stall with smoke glass was large enough for two people to fit comfortably. "No we wouldn't have."

Bryson glanced over at the shower and back at her. "You're probably right. I'll go start breakfast."

The naked desire in his eyes almost made her call him back. Raven brushed her teeth and took a quick shower. She wrapped the towel around her and went back to the bedroom where she found her underwear on the chair with her dress. She didn't want to put the dress back on, so she wrapped the towel around her and called down to Bryson.

He appeared at the bedroom door a moment later. "What do you need?"

"I need something to wear."

Bryson opened a drawer, took out a T-shirt and handed it to her.

She put it on and, although it hit her mid-thigh, she felt naked wearing just her panties. "Do you have a pair of shorts?"

"My shorts are not going to fit you." He opened another drawer, pulled out a pair of basketball shorts and held them up. "See?"

Raven snatched them. "I'll just tie them tighter." Even after tying and folding them over twice, they still hit her at the knees.

He burst out laughing.

Scowling, she marched past him and went downstairs to the kitchen. He followed, still laughing. Smoked sausage sat on a paper towel and eggs were in a bowl waiting to be cooked.

Bryson turned on the skillet. "How many pieces of toast do you want?"

"Just one." He dropped the bread in the toaster, added butter to the pan, waited for it to melt and poured in the eggs. She observed him moving around the kitchen with ease and efficiency, timing it so both were done at the same time.

"Can you get plates?"

She went over to the cabinets and took down plates. She'd been to his house so many times since he purchased it three years ago, she knew where everything was almost as well as he did. They fixed their plates and sat at the bar to eat. Bryson went to the refrigerator and poured a glass of orange juice for her and milk for him. He didn't have to ask because he knew her. She thought about Darren. They had dated for four months and he'd never once asked what she liked or stepped foot in a kitchen to cook her breakfast or dinner. She should have kicked him to the curb long before she did.

After breakfast, she helped Bryson clean the kitchen. He folded the towel and asked, "What do you want to do today?"

"I don't know. I need to go home and get some clothes."

Bryson angled his head thoughtfully. "I don't know. I kind of like what you're wearing." He wiggled his eyebrows.

Raven snorted. "You are such a man."

He flexed his biceps. "All man, baby. And don't you forget it."

"You call those little bitty things muscles?" she teased. She took one look at his face and took off running.

He caught her in three strides and scooped her into his arms. "I'll show you little bitty muscles." He tossed her in the air and caught her.

She screamed. "If you drop me, I'm gonna kick your butt, Bryson Allen Montgomery."

"You're the one talking about my muscles, Raven Antoinette Holloway." He lifted her above his head. "You were saying?"

"Put me down! Okay, okay, your muscles aren't itty bitty."

He lowered her to her feet. "That's what I thought."

She hit him in the chest and ran through the family room and up the stairs with him on her heels. She tried to close the bedroom door, but he was too strong.

He grabbed her around the waist and tossed her onto the bed. "So you want to play?"

His play turned out to be the most erotic and passionate game she'd ever engaged in and when it ended, she was sated and smiling.

* * *

Monday evening, Raven only wanted to take a shower and curl up in bed. Whenever she felt overwhelmed, she had to shut down for a while so her mind and body could process things. However, as soon as she walked through the door, Simeon called. She seriously contemplated letting it go to voicemail, but didn't want to risk him showing up on her doorstep, instead.

"Yes, Simeon," she said when she connected.

"You have five minutes to tell me what's going on between you and Bryson or I will be camping out at your house until you talk."

"No hello, how was your day?"

Simeon remained silent.

Raven fell across the bed and groaned. "We're dating, okay?"

"I knew something was different. You don't *ever* wear a dress and I don't recall him staring at you the way he was last Saturday. All I have to say is if he hurts you, his ass is mine. And, yeah, I know you're the big sister, but you're still my sister and I love you."

She cursed under her breath. Why did he have to go and get all sentimental? "I love you, too," she mumbled.

"The only reason I'm letting you off easy is because I've seen how he's treated you all these years. Bryson is a good guy."

"Thanks, Simeon. Bryse is definitely one of the good guys." Though she would never admit it, her brother's endorsement meant everything to her.

"I do have one question."

"What?" she asked warily.

"What happened to the other guy you were dating? Not that I'm complaining because he struck me as a pompous jerk."

"He was a pompous jerk."

Simeon laughed. "You can tell me the story some other time. I gotta go. I have to be at the office at six in the morning."

"You've been working a lot of hours, baby bro. You're going to burnout before your career gets started."

He sighed heavily. "I know. But this what I need to do to establish myself."

"I get that. Just don't overdo it."

"I won't. Oh, and tell Bryson, he and I will talk soon about his intentions. Night, sis."

"Night." Raven tossed the phone on the bed. She already knew Bryson's intentions. He'd made them very clear.

* * *

Tuesday afternoon, Bryson sat in his office smiling. He couldn't remember the last time he'd been so happy. Yes, he could. College. He thought about Delaney and how much he had loved her then. However, it didn't compare to the deep emotional connection he had with Raven. He realized his feelings for Delaney were that of a young man barely out of his teens who had no idea what it really meant to be in love. Now, he did.

"Still smiling, huh?" Jerome said, coming into the office and sprawling in one of the chairs.

"Yep."

"Those were some pretty serious words about Raven last Friday."

He leaned back in his chair. "They were. And it surprised the hell out of me to hear them coming from my mouth."

"So, you're not that serious about her then?"

"Oh, no, I'm very serious."

Jerome cocked his head to the side. "How serious?"

"I'm in love with her."

"Whoa. Love? You sure this isn't some built-up emotions from over the years?"

"Positive. We'd always been dating other people, so it wasn't something that ever crossed my mind in all the years we've been friends."

"I'm just…wow. Since you're serious, so am I."

Bryson frowned. "About what?"

"About being the best man."

"Well, if she says yes, you can have the job."

Jerome leaned forward and held up both hands. "Okay, wait. I need you to slow down. Are you talking about asking Raven to marry you…*soon*?"

"Yes."

He scrubbed a hand over his forehead. "Bryse, you've only been dating her like what? A month?"

"Close to it," Bryson answered mildly. He knew what he wanted and didn't see the need to wait forever.

"Look, man. Don't you think you're moving a little too fast?"

"No. Rome, you'd have a point if I'd just met Raven. It's not like we need to take time to get to know each other. We've been friends for twelve years and I know her almost as well as I know myself."

"Okay, I'll concede you that point, but what about Raven?"

"She told me she loved me." And the words had been playing in his head like the melody to his favorite song.

Jerome stared in disbelief. "I thought she was having a hard time accepting this." He rose to his feet and paced in front of Bryson. "And you plan to ask her when?"

"Hopefully, tomorrow."

He spun around. "I can't even process this right now."

Bryson chuckled. "Good thing you don't have to. I know it seems fast, but I know it's right. I love her."

"Then that's all that matters." They shared a brotherly hug. "Ken is *not* going to believe this."

"I'm sure you'll fill him in."

"You'd better believe it. I was going to text, but I think this deserves a phone call. Later."

Bryson smiled. Even though they didn't always agree, his boys had his back. He pulled out his phone and texted Raven, asking her to call when she had a chance. She called back twenty minutes later.

"Hey, Bryse," she said when he answered.

"Hey, baby. I know you're working, so I won't keep you. I just wanted to know if I could stop by after work tomorrow."

"I'm supposed to be having dinner with a couple of my coworkers, but I can come by your place afterward. Should be no later than nine."

"That works. I'll talk to you later."

"Okay."

He disconnected and smiled. He had some shopping to do.

# Chapter Ten

Wednesday evening, Bryson placed the strawberries he had just dipped in milk and white chocolate into the refrigerator next to the bottle of Raven's favorite Ballatore champagne. She'd always said it doesn't have to be expensive to taste good. He had planned to take her to dinner, but since she was already going out, he'd just provide the dessert. She rarely ordered dessert whenever she went out, citing the need to let her food digest for at least an hour before eating anything else. She hadn't changed in all the years he had known her.

Just as he'd told Jerome, he knew her inside out, her likes and dislikes and unconscious habits—tapping her left index finger when she was thinking, or tilting her head slightly to the right and biting her bottom lip when she was angry.

The doorbell rang. Bryson surveyed the family room to make sure everything was in place, hit *play* on his iPod and then went to let Raven in.

He hauled her into his arms and slanted his mouth over hers before she could get cross the threshold. He lifted her off her feet, kicked the door shut and carried her to the family room. Bryson let her slide down his body until her feet hit the floor and smiled at her. "Hi." She still had on her slacks and polo from work and her hair was pulled back in the standard ponytail she wore during the week, but to him, she was the most beautiful woman he'd ever seen.

Raven returned his smile. "Hi." She glanced around. "Wow.

It's lovely."

He had lit vanilla fragranced candles around the room, placed a blanket covered with rose petals in the center of the floor and turned on the electric fireplace. He'd left the air conditioner on, however.

"A girl can get used to this."

"I hope so. A queen should always be treated as such, even if she's one of the guys," Bryson added teasingly.

She laughed softly. "Well, as long as you don't mess up my tough girl image, it's all good."

"Your image is safe with me." He kissed her again, slowly, seductively, tangling their tongues together in a dance meant only for lovers. He lifted his head and traced a finger down her cheek. "Make yourself comfortable on the blanket. I'll be right back."

Raven placed her purse on the end table and removed her shoes.

The doorbell rang again. "Can you get that?" Bryson called from the kitchen. He'd asked his jeweler friend to come by. He retrieved the champagne, glasses and strawberries and headed back to the family room. He froze upon seeing Whitney standing there.

"My, my, isn't this cozy." Whitney looked Raven up and down.

"What are you doing here, Whitney?" Raven had a mixture of hurt and anger on her face and Bryson wanted to shake Whitney for showing up out of the blue. She had never come to his house without calling first.

"I was in the neighborhood and thought we could catch up on old times."

He didn't miss the emphasis she had placed on *old times*. And neither did Raven, if her expression was any indication.

Raven stuck her feet into her shoes and snatched up her purse. "Then I'll let you two catch up." She walked out without a backwards glance.

Bryson set down everything in his hands and went after her. She was already at her car when he got outside. "Raven, wait." He reached for her and she held up a hand.

"I don't think I can do this right now, Bryson."

"I don't know why she's here."

"Oh, didn't you hear her? She came so you two can catch up on old times," she said sarcastically. "Sorry." Raven scrubbed a hand across her forehead. "Look, I need some time. I have to go."

"Listen to me, dammit! I haven't seen or spoken to her in over six months and we were never in a relationship. You know I would never do anything like this to you. I love you, Raven." He could see the tears standing in her eyes and he wanted to take her in his arms, but didn't want to risk upsetting her any further.

She got into the car, started the engine and roared off.

He cursed again and strode back inside, slamming the door. Whitney was eating a strawberry when he walked into the family room and his anger boiled over. He grabbed the bowl. "Again, what are you doing here?"

Whitney gave him a sexy laugh. "If I didn't know better, I'd think you weren't glad to see me."

"Give the woman a prize. We haven't spoken in over six months."

She brushed past him and surveyed the room. "This really is a lovely set up."

It would have been lovelier had she not made an appearance. He needed to talk to Raven, and the sooner the better. As it stood, he was afraid they were going to be back at square one, or worse. Whitney came toward him with an exaggerated switch in her hips and tried to press her body against his. He took two steps back. She had come dressed for seduction in a fire engine red dress that molded to her curves. In the past, it might have turned him on, but he felt nothing tonight. Except anger.

"I'm only going to be in town a couple of days and since we're alone now," she waved a hand around the room, "no need to let all this go to waste. I do have to say that I'm a little disappointed that you never went through all this trouble whenever we got together."

"You and I didn't have that type of relationship. She and I do." He saw the moment she finally understood.

Whitney chuckled bitterly. "So, you're telling me that all of a sudden you're a one-woman man now."

"That's exactly what I'm telling you. And had you called beforehand, I would've explained that to you. I'm sorry, Whitney, but I can't see you anymore."

She ran her hand over her body. "You're willing to give all this up for a fling?"

"What I'm willing to do is give my all to the woman I love." Bryson escorted her to the door.

She jerked away from him. "Well, I hope the two of you make it." Her tone suggested anything but.

"Goodbye, Whitney." He closed the door and leaned his head against it. His world had gone to hell in less than five minutes. He turned and the bell rang again. *What now?* He snatched the door open.

"What's up, Bryson?" His jeweler friend, Myles Hudson stood there smiling.

Bryson groaned. He quickly explained the situation.

"I'm sorry to hear that. I hope you can get everything straightened out."

"Thanks. I will." They shook hands and Bryson watched him walk away. He had to get it straight. He was *not* going to lose her.

* * *

Raven bit her lip to keep the tears from falling as she drove. She should have known better. And it hurt even more because she trusted Bryson. What made it worse was she didn't know who to talk to because he'd always been the person she ran to when she had problems. She contemplated going over to Erika's, but changed her mind because of the late hour.

Twenty minutes later, she ended up at her brother's house.

"Raven. What are you doing here?" Simeon asked, clearly

shocked. He moved back so she could enter. "Come in."

She stopped short upon seeing a woman lounging comfortably on the sofa. "Oh, I'm sorry. I didn't know you had company. I'll just talk to you tomorrow." She turned to leave.

Simeon placed a staying hand on her arm, concern evident in his face. "You're not leaving. Give me a minute." He went over and spoke quietly to the woman. She nodded. He came back with the woman. "Andrea, this is my sister, Raven. Raven, Andrea."

Andrea smiled warmly and extended her hand. "It's so nice to meet you, Raven. I've heard many good things about you."

Raven shot a quick glance at her brother. She couldn't say the same, so she smiled instead. "Nice meeting you, too."

"Let me see Andrea out and I'll be right back."

She nodded and dropped down on the sofa. How could Bryse do this to her? Okay, he seemed shocked, but the woman wouldn't just pop up unless they had history.

"Okay, sis. What's going on?"

"While I was at Bryson's house, a woman showed up." She explained what happened. "I felt like a complete fool. I believed him, trusted him." The tears threatened to fall, but she forced them back.

Simeon studied her. "Has he ever brought her name up?"

"No."

"Yet he's talked about his girlfriends in the past."

"Yeah," she said slowly, not sure where he was going.

"You're not going to like what I have to say, but if he never said anything, then she wasn't worth mentioning."

Raven jumped to her feet and strode angrily toward the door. "You men are all alike."

Simeon cut her off and placed his hands on her shoulders. "Hear me out, sis. I know you're angry with Bryson, but from what you've told me, he would've never invited that woman, knowing you were coming."

Her shoulders sagged and those damn tears came anyway.

He peered into her face. "Raven, I truly believe that what he had with her was nothing more than a casual once-in-a-while type arrangement. You said you knew about all his ex's, right?"

She nodded.

"Met them?"

"Yes," she mumbled.

"When was the last one?"

Raven thought back and couldn't remember. Was it last year?

Simeon wiped her tears. "I rest my case," he said softly and kissed her forehead. He hugged her. "You love him, don't you?"

"Yes," she whispered on a broken sob. The tears came full force and she let herself be consoled by the little boy who she had always taken care of, who now eclipsed her height by six inches and who had become a man of whom she was extremely proud. When the tears finally stopped, she looked up at her brother. "I thought this was supposed to be my job."

He smiled. "It still is, but it's okay if we switch up every now and then."

She gave him a watery smile. "Thank you. I'm sorry for interrupting your date."

"It's okay. Andrea's cool. She's an attorney I met recently. We're both trying to work our way up in our firms."

"Well, I'd better go."

"Stay. We can watch *Captain America* and I'll make you popcorn with extra butter and an orange freeze."

He knew she wouldn't be able to resist. "Okay." He went to make popcorn and Raven removed her shoes and sat on the sofa. Had he been right about Bryson? Bryson said he hadn't seen her in months, but the woman waltzed into his home like she owned the place and it had infuriated Raven to no end. Most people would probably call it jealousy and she probably would, too if she owned up to it, which she wouldn't. Maybe she wasn't ready for the type of relationship Bryson offered. Life was so much simpler when they were just friends. She heard a buzzing sound and glanced around. It took a moment to realize it was her phone. Raven dug it out of her purse and saw the missed call from Bryson. Actually five missed calls. She didn't want talk to him right now. She knew he wouldn't stop calling and wouldn't put it past him to camp out at her house, and she couldn't deal with all the emotions right now. *What am I going to do?* A thought came to her. Home. She could go home.

Simeon entered with a big bowl of popcorn and two orange freezes. He handed her a glass and sat down next to her. He picked up the remote, turned the television on and started the movie from the On Demand menu.

"I think I want to go home for a few days."

"Ah, okay. What about work?"

"I don't know. Say I have a family emergency or something."

"Are you serious about wanting to go?"

"Yes."

"Then I'll make the reservation and you can leave tomorrow."

"Okay." She had never run from anything in her life—that had always been Ryleigh's thing. A small voice in her head reminded her that Ryleigh had found her forever when she stopped running, but Raven ignored it. Raven typically faced her problems head-on, but this time she was running as far away as she could.

# Chapter Eleven

Bryson was at his wits end. He had a hundred things to do today at the center, but he couldn't concentrate on even one. He'd called Raven a half a dozen times last night and sat outside her place until one in the morning and she hadn't come home. She wouldn't return his calls and he was close to losing his mind. *Where is she?* He braced his hands on his desk and bowed his head. His heart felt like it had been ripped out of his chest. He drew in a deep breath.

"No word from Raven?" He lifted his head and saw Jerome standing in the doorway of his office.

He shook his head. "She won't return my calls."

Jerome came in and shut the door. "Maybe you should try her job."

"I already called. She didn't come in." He collapsed into his chair and dragged a hand down his face. "What am I going to do, Rome? I love her so much it hurts. I need to find her and try to talk to her." He let out an animalistic growl. "Where the hell is she?"

Jerome pulled out his phone and made a call. After a moment, he put it back in his pocket. She's not answering. A knock sounded and he opened the door. "Hey, Ken."

Kendrick came in. "Anything?"

"No," Bryson answered in an agonized whisper. Both his friends wore expressions of concern. He'd called last night and told them about the disastrous events that had occurred.

"She's not answering my calls, either," Jerome said.

Kendrick sighed. "Same here. Bryse, have you thought about calling her brother?"

"Simeon?" Would she have gone to him? And if she had, would Simeon tell Bryson? "No. I don't have his number, but Raven mentioned where he worked once."

Jerome and Kendrick shared a look. "Call him," they said.

"She's his sister and he probably won't tell me anything if he thinks I hurt her."

"Maybe, maybe not," Kendrick said. "But if you love Raven like you say you do, I figure you'll do whatever it takes to get her back."

"I do." He rotated his chair toward his laptop and googled the name of the law firm. Once he had the number, he called and a receptionist informed him that Simeon was out unavailable at the moment, but had an opening for a consultation that afternoon due to a cancellation. Bryson scheduled the appointment and hung up. He looked at Jerome and Kendrick's expectant gazes. "I have an appointment with Simeon at two." He just wished he could be sure that he would come away with the information he needed.

The day seemed to creep by and he became more anxious the closer it came to the time he had to leave. At one o'clock, he powered off his laptop, locked it in the drawer and went to find Jerome. He found him in one of the classrooms observing the first and second grade summer school class. Bryson got Jerome's attention and signaled for him to step out. "I just want to let you know I'm leaving." The drive to the Wilshire District should take only thirty-five or forty minutes, but LA traffic could be unpredictable and he'd rather be early than late.

"Okay. Are you coming back?"

"Depends on what I find out."

Jerome clapped him on the back. "Good luck, my brother."

"Thanks. I'm going to need it."

As he suspected, the congested street and highways added ten minutes to his driving time and he arrived with eight minutes to spare. He parked in the underground garage and followed the directions to the fourth-floor office. A woman sat at the receptionist desk and greeted him.

"Hello. I have an appointment with Simeon Holloway."

She pulled up a screen on her computer and searched for a minute. "Mr. Montgomery?"

"Yes."

"Have a seat and I'll let Mr. Holloway know you're here."

"Thank you." Bryson sat in one of the leather chairs in the waiting room and did something he hadn't done in a long time. He prayed.

"Bryson."

His eyes popped open and swiftly came to his feet. "Simeon."

"Come on back."

He followed Simeon past several offices and stopped at one midway down the hall.

Simeon closed the door and gestured Bryson to a chair. "I assume you're here about Raven."

"If you know that, then she told you what happened. Believe me, I was angrier than Raven about Whitney."

He nodded.

"I need to talk to her. She's not returning my calls, she's not at home or at work."

"Do you love my sister?"

He met Simeon's challenging stare unflinchingly. "More than life itself. You've never seen me mistreat your sister and I never will."

Simeon regarded Bryson silently. "For what it's worth, I believe you."

Bryson released the breath he'd been holding. "Do you know where she is?"

"Yes. Since you and my sister are good friends, you have to

know that relationships have always been hard for her. Men don't always know how to take her because she's not afraid of speaking her mind. Raven has a handle on every area in her life, except this one. She retreats at the first sign of trouble. It's how she protects herself."

"I know. But I would never hurt her. She means too much to me. I need to know where she is, Simeon. Please."

Simeon seemed to struggle with whether to tell Bryson her whereabouts or not. "And when you find her?"

"Do what I had planned to do last night. Ask her to marry me," Bryson answered without hesitation.

"I've always respected you, Bryson and if I didn't know your history with Raven, I'd let you take your chances. But I want my sister to be happy and I know she loves you, too. Just don't hurt her," he said warningly.

"You have my word."

"She went home."

Stunned, Bryson asked, "South Carolina?"

"Yes. She'll be back on Monday." A smile played around the corners of Simeon's mouth. "The look on your face says you don't want to wait that long."

"I can't." Today was Thursday and no way would he make it another four days without trying to make things right. "Where's the nearest hotel in Rosewood Heights?"

He rounded his desk, wrote something on a piece of paper and handed it to Bryson.

"Rosewood Inn?"

"Yeah. There are a few large chain hotels outside of Rosewood Heights, but this is the best place to stay."

"Thanks, Simeon." Bryson felt the weight on his chest ease a fraction. "I'll be there late tonight or tomorrow, depending on when I can get a flight." He retrieved a business card and gave it to Simeon. "Here's my number. Do you think you can find out where Raven will be tomorrow?"

Simeon chuckled. "Probably either at the town's bakery or the gardens at Rosewood Estates. Those are her favorite places. I'll call her tomorrow around noon to be sure, then let you know."

"I appreciate this, man." He extended his hand and Simeon grasped it in a firm handshake.

"Just make Raven happy and promise me you won't be a bossy big brother."

Bryson smiled for the first time. "Done. Raven is bossy enough for the both of us."

"True that."

He was searching for flights on his phone before he exited the elevator and found that the earliest available wouldn't be until tonight. Once in the car, he called Jerome, filled him in and told him that he wouldn't be back until Monday. He wasn't leaving without Raven. He made a second call to Myles. It was time to go get his woman.

* * *

Raven felt her stress melt away the moment Ava drove into the town limits. "Thanks for picking me up."

"Oh, girl, you know I would've been upset if you had called anyone else. I do have to say I was pretty surprised to get your call this morning."

"I just needed to get away for a few days."

"Who hurt you?"

She should have expected the question. "Can we talk about it later?"

"Whenever you're ready. You want to go to your parents' house?"

Raven would have preferred to stay at the Rosewood Inn, but her mother would have a heart attack. "I guess. But can we stop at Roseberry Bakery? I need some butter cookies." Mrs. Oak's butter cookies and blueberry muffins drew crowds from all over the state. Growing up, she and her girlfriends had visited the bakery at least once a week.

Ava laughed. "I might need to get a couple myself." She

turned down the street leading to downtown and, minutes later, parked in front of the bakery.

The familiar smells of the bakery hit Raven's nose and an involuntary moan slipped out. She greeted the people she knew and placed her order, limiting herself to only half a dozen. She could eat double that amount in one sitting, but at thirty, the weight didn't come off as easy anymore. She'd eaten two cookies by the time they got back into the car. "I can't believe they still taste exactly the same as when we were kids."

"I know, right? These things are addictive. I really have to watch it. Gotta keep it sexy for Owen."

Raven smiled. "How is married life?"

"Absolutely fabulous."

Raven was happy for Ava, but it only served to magnify the pain in her heart and the knowledge that she would never have the same.

Ava seemed to sense the change and said, "I'll come by later and we can talk."

"Okay." A few minutes later, Ava parked in front of her parents' house. Home. She leaned over and hugged her friend. "See you in a while." She got out, retrieved her suitcase from the backseat and rolled it up the walk.

Her mother came barreling out of the house and down the steps toward her. "Oh, my goodness! Raven." She grabbed her up and held Raven like she would never let go.

"Hi, Mom." Tears stung her eyes.

She held Raven away, gave her a once over then pulled her into another crushing hug. "Why didn't you tell me you were coming? How long are you staying? Have you eaten?"

Raven laughed. "Can I answer one question at a time? I'll be here until Monday morning and I had two butter cookies on the way. I just needed to be home for a few days."

Her mother studied her critically. "Well, come on in, baby. I sense you need some cheering up. Your daddy's going to be so happy to see you."

"Is he home yet?"

"He got here five minutes ago."

She carried her bag up the steps and into the house.

"Margaret, who are you talking to—" His eyes lit up. "Hey, baby girl."

Her father rushed over and, once again, Raven was swept up in a hug. She basked in the strong embrace of her father. She had always been a daddy's girl and no one gave hugs like him. "Hi, Daddy."

"Why didn't you tell us you were coming?"

"I just wanted to come home for a few days." Her parents shared a glance. "What? I can't come home?"

"Of course you can. Go put your stuff in your room and come on out to the porch so we can talk. And welcome home, baby."

Raven smiled. She headed to her room. When she got there, she stood in the middle of the floor and drew in a deep, calming breath. This was exactly what she needed. She quickly changed into a tank top and shorts and walked barefoot out to the front porch. Her parents were sitting in their favorite swing with glasses of sweet tea. Raven picked up the third glass and sat in the rocking chair facing the swing.

"How's the job going?" her father asked.

"It's going well. Just busy, as usual. Simeon said you two are thinking of going on a cruise."

"We're more than thinking about it," her mother said with a smile. "We booked it for September."

"That's wonderful. Where are you going?"

"It's a week-long cruise to the Caribbean."

A twinge of envy hit Raven as she watched her parents share a loving stare and a short kiss. Memories of Bryson's kiss rose so sharply in her mind, she could almost feel his lips against hers. Her eyes slid closed.

"Raven, are you okay, honey?"

She opened her eyes and smiled at her mother. "I'm fine. Just a little tired from the flight." She set the tea aside. She asked them more about the cruise and caught up on all her family and friends. Soon her parents went back inside, her mother to start dinner and her father to take a phone call. Raven relished the quiet, lush green surroundings. She could sit out here all night.

As promised, Ava came back. She went in to speak to Raven's parents then came back out to the porch. "You ready to talk about it?"

"No, but I'll tell you anyway." She started with the breakup with Darren, Bryson consoling her and the two of them ending up in bed together, and finished with their subsequent relationship and the devastating events that led her back to her hometown.

"So do you think he was cheating on you?"

Over the past twenty-four hours, Raven had done a lot of thinking and had come to the conclusion that Bryson had been truthful about not having seen Whitney in months. "No."

"Then why haven't you talked to him?"

"Scared, I guess. It's crazy, I know. Me, the queen of the daredevils, ran clear across the country because I'm afraid to let go."

"Raven, love means taking the risk, even though you're afraid. Imagine your life with Bryson."

Raven thought about all the years he'd been part of her life—the laughter, fun, the serious times, and more recently, last weekend at his house. She smiled.

"Now imagine it without him."

Her heart almost stopped and she struggled to draw in a breath. Bryson had been such an integral part of her life she couldn't envision him not being there. "I can't." A pain spread across her chest and she brought her hand up and massaged the spot, hoping to ease the agony.

"I didn't think so. Stop running, Raven. I know Mac, Ryleigh and Quinn would tell you the same thing."

Once again, Quinn's words floated across her mind. *Don't let your fears stop you from being happy because I believe he could be the one for you.* "I don't know how."

Ava grasped her hand. "Just let go. I promise it'll all work out."

Ava sounded so sure. Raven wished she shared her optimism.

* * *

Bryson followed Simeon's directions and spotted the man holding the sign with his name.

"Welcome to South Carolina, Mr. Montgomery."

"Thank you."

"Do you have any other bags?"

"No, just this one." He had brought one carry on because he didn't want to waste one minute longer than he had to before seeing Raven.

"Then follow me."

The man led him to a black Town Car parked at the curb. Bryson got in and leaned his head back. He was exhausted from the overnight flight because he hadn't been able to sleep. Would she be happy to see him or would he be going back home without the woman he loved and his best friend? The drive to Rosewood Heights took just over an hour and a pretty, young woman with skin the color of light brown sugar and dark, sparkling eyes smiled at him from behind the long mahogany counter at the Rosewood Inn. He gave her his name, identification and credit card.

"Mr. Montgomery, welcome to Rosewood Heights. We have you reserved for three nights."

"Thank you and yes."

"It's a little early for check-in, but let me see if I have something available." She clicked a few keys.

Bryson glanced down at his watch. Ten forty-five. He hoped they had a room. He would pay the extra cost if necessary.

"You're in luck. I do have a room with one king-sized bed." She handed him his ID and credit card, along with the room key. “The restaurant serves breakfast until eleven thirty. The waffles are to die for,” she added with a smile. “Phillip will show you to your room.” She gestured to a bellhop standing nearby.

He followed Phillip to a second floor room that had a balcony overlooking the gardens. The inn had all the charm of a small town, from the airy room with a ceiling fan, to the wrought iron surrounding the balcony.

Bryson felt rejuvenated after his shower. He decided to wait until later to unpack. He put the room key in his pocket, took the stairs down to the first floor to the small restaurant.

After placing his order, he sat back and contemplated how to get Raven back. The only thing he could do was tell her what lay in his heart. He just hoped Simeon came through with the information Bryson needed and that everything turned out in his favor.

# *Chapter Twelve*

"So have you thought any more about talking to Bryson?" Ava asked Raven Friday as they walked through the gardens at Rosewood Estates.

"A little." Truthfully, Raven had thought of nothing else all night. "But I have no idea what I would say." She stopped walking and scanned the fence with all the locks. There were far more than she remembered seeing last year. "I guess a lot of people are finding love." Whenever a couple got engaged or expressed their love in the garden, they placed a lock on the fence.

"There've been four more weddings here since mine. Maybe yours will be next."

She gave Ava a sidelong glance. "I don't think so." But, secretly, she wouldn't mind being married next to the lake. At sunset, the view was unlike anything she'd ever seen.

"Just tell him what you feel."

It took a second to realize Ava had picked up on their previous conversation. "Everything is so jumbled up. Each time I think a relationship is going to be good, I end up being wrong and this time…" She let the sentence hang. She couldn't bring herself to say out loud that this time she didn't want to be wrong. She wanted it to be good forever.

A smile blossomed on Ava's face. "I have a feeling you won't be wrong this time."

Raven eyed her. "How do you know?"

Ava shrugged. “From what I remember about him, he seemed like a great guy.”

Raven’s cell rang. She glanced down at the display and saw her brother’s name. “Let me answer this. Hey, Simeon.”

“Hey, sis. I just wanted to check on you.”

She smiled. “I’m good. Just sitting in Love’s Last Garden, talking to Ava.”

“Well, I won’t hold you. Tell Ava I said hello. See you when you get back home.”

“Okay. I’ll tell her.” She disconnected. “Simeon said hi.”

“Did he get his case handled?”

“Yes. But I worry about him putting in so many hours. Just like someone else I know,” she added, smiling at Ava. Ava served on almost every committee in town, was involved in the town planning and often acted as the personal assistant to the mayor. Raven still didn’t know her actual job title.

Ava laughed. ”Hey, there’s a lot to do. Actually, I’ve slowed down a little. I have something else to occupy my time now.”

“Mmm hmm, I bet. Owen is probably the only person who can slow you down.”

“You’re probably right.”

Raven just shook her head. They continued to converse while sitting on a bench beneath a large oak tree. Raven took in the beauty of the area—sunflowers, coneflowers, hydrangeas, and, of course, a few Carolina Jessamines, the state flower. Thankfully, the humidity hadn’t climbed to unbearable levels as yet, but the late June temperatures were expected to be near ninety.

“Hey, beautiful.”

Raven whirled around so fast she almost fell off the bench. “*Bryson?* What…what are you doing here?” Her heart started pounding in her chest. He looked so good it took everything in her not to leap into his arms. Evidently he’d checked the weather because he had on beige shorts, a pale blue silk tee and leather sandals. No one wore dark colors at this time of the year.

"Guess I'm not the only one whose nights are going to be occupied," Ava said just loud enough for Raven to hear her. She stood and extended her hand. "I don't know if you remember me, but I'm Ava."

Bryson clasped her hand. "I do. It's good to see you again and congratulations on your marriage."

"Thank you. Well, I'll leave you two to talk." Ava divided an amused glance between Raven and Bryson and hurried off. When she was behind Bryson, she caught Raven's gaze, held up her phone and mouthed, "Call me later."

Raven nodded. She turned her attention back to Bryson. "You never answered my question."

"I came for you. May I?" Bryson gestured to the bench.

She nodded and scooted over. For a moment he didn't say anything. She had a thousand questions, starting with who had told him she'd come home and how he knew where she would be.

"I'm sorry I hurt you, Raven."

A measure of guilt rose. "You didn't hurt me, Bryson. I believe you didn't know about Whitney's plans."

"I met her about a year and a half ago at a business conference and we ended up in her hotel room. She's a recruiter for her job in Seattle and came through LA a lot. We got together a few times for dinner or drinks, but that's it. I never mentioned her to you because we never had a relationship. The last time I had spoken with her was when she called to say Happy New Year."

Simeon had said the same thing and she felt worse. "I'm sorry."

Bryson faced her. "Baby, why didn't you wait and let me explain?"

"Because what I feel for you scares me so much. In every relationship I've had, what started out as being good turned to bad and I don't think I could handle that if it happens to us."

"Sweetheart, listen to me. I know your history, just like you know mine. We've both had some bad things happen in relationships. But do you know what? Through all of them, one thing remained good."

"What?"

"Us."

Raven searched his face. Every moment of their twelve years together flashed in her mind. He was right. "Oh my God, Bryse. I'm so sorry." The tears came.

He smiled and draped his arm around her. "You don't have to apologize, Raven. I know that you're afraid. But I also know that you love me. I can feel it here." He pointed to his heart. "Let go of your fears. You told me you trusted me with your life. Trust me with your heart, baby and I promise to take good care of it."

She placed her hand on his heart and felt the strong, steady beat. "You always have." The fact that he had come all the way to South Carolina proved how far he was willing to go for her. Now, she had to show him how far she would go for him, to prove that she was ready to embrace all he had to offer. "I'm ready, Bryse."

"For what?"

"To embrace everything you're offering."

Bryson held out his hand. "What I'm offering you is forever."

Raven hesitated for the briefest of moments before placing her hand in his. She trusted him and he had never let her down. "I love you, Bryse."

"I love you, too. Forever."

She kissed him, pouring into it everything he made her feel.

He picked her up, straddled her on his lap and rested his forehead against hers. "I was so worried about you. And when you weren't at home or work, I almost lost my mind. You didn't answer any of our calls."

Once again, her guilt surfaced. Bryson, Jerome and Kendrick had called several times and left messages. "I know and I'm sorry. I'll call them later."

"*We'll* call them later. I'm just happy to have you in my

arms again. Promise me that you won't do this again. I don't think my heart could take not knowing where you are."

"I promise. No more running."

Bryson stared at her intently, understanding the gravity of her words. "Unless you're running to me. I will always be there to catch you."

Something burst free in her heart. "And you'd better not drop me."

He roared with laughter.

Raven just smiled. She wrapped her arms around him and laid her head on his shoulder. He was hers. "How long are you staying?"

"I'm flying home with you Monday morning."

Her head came up. Only one person knew her flight information. "Simeon. He told you?"

"He did. But he made me promise two things first—to make you happy and to not turn into a bossy big brother."

"And you said?"

"That I had no problems making you happy and I wouldn't turn into that kind of brother because you're bossy enough for the both of us."

"You what?" she asked with mock outrage, punching him in the chest.

"Ow!" Bryson rubbed the spot.

"You're lucky that's all I did." She rolled her eyes and climbed off his lap.

Bryson stood. "Don't be mad. You know we love you."

"Whatever," she muttered, trying to hide her smile.

He reached for her hand. "Let's go for a walk. This is a beautiful place."

"It is. My favorite spot is down by the lake." They set off on a leisurely stroll and Raven shared all the historical points. Later, she received a text from Ava: *From the sound of all that laughter coming from the garden, I assume all is well. He's a keeper!* She laughed.

"What's so funny?"

"Nothing really. Ava just texted me." Raven's stomach growled softly. "Do you want to go get something to eat?"

"I had waffles at the Rosewood Inn earlier and I'm not that hungry, but what did you have in mind?"

"Ooh, those waffles will make you hurt somebody, they're so good. Is that where you're staying?"

"Yes. I can't convince you to come stay with me, can I?" Bryson gently nipped at her ear. "I'll make it well worth it."

She was tempted, oh so tempted. But this was a small town and word would spread like a wild fire if she "shacked up" with him. "I would love to, but my parents would go ballistic. Speaking of my parents, they'll want to see you." They'd met Bryson when she graduated from college. "I was going to suggest going to the Little Rose Café for lunch, but if my mother finds out that the townsfolk saw you before she did—and the word *will* beat us back to the house—I'll never live it down."

"Well, I don't want to mess up with your mother, so…" He gestured her forward.

"I'm certain she'll be more than happy to whip something up, and I don't mean sandwiches and chips." Raven was also certain that her mother would go absolutely crazy over Bryson. They walked back through the estate to the lot where she had parked her mother's car and she drove them the ten minutes to her parents' house.

"I like the porch. Looks like a great place to sit at the end of the day."

"That's exactly what I did." She held his hand as they climbed the steps to the front door. "Mom," Raven called, entering.

"I'm right—" Her mother stopped short upon seeing Bryson and a look of wonder bloomed on her face. "Hello, I'm Margaret Holloway." Then recognition dawned. "Bryson? Oh, my goodness. I didn't recognize you with your new hairstyle." She came over, hugged him and took both his hands.

"Hello, Mrs. Holloway. It's good to see you again."

He unleashed his smile and Raven thought her mother would swoon right there. "You can let go of him now, Mom." She shook her head.

"Bryson, Raven didn't tell me you were coming. What brings you to our little beach town?"

"Raven." Bryson answered her mother, but his eyes were on Raven. "We had a little misunderstanding and I came to clear the air and to let her know that I love her and she will always be first in my life."

Her mother gasped and brought both hands to her mouth. "Are you telling me you're together, *together?* More than friends?"

He smiled over at Raven and she said, "Yes, Mom. That's what we're saying."

"*Hallelujah!* Thank you, Lord for answering my prayer." She grabbed Bryson in one of her famous crushing hugs. "I am so happy!" She finally turned him loose. "Are you hungry? Let me go fix you all some lunch. Raven, take Bryson out to the porch and I'll let you know when it's ready. Oh, your father is going to be so surprised. I've got to go call him." She started for the kitchen and stopped. "I'm just so happy." She hurried off.

Raven shook her head and did as her mother said. She sat on the swing and patted the space next to her.

Bryson sat and pulled her close. "Your mom is sweet."

"My mom is a mess," she countered, laughing.

He chuckled and set the swing to a slow sway.

"You know, I always envied the time my parents spent sitting here together. I wondered how it would feel to sit just like this with someone I love. I don't have to wonder anymore."

"And how does it feel?"

"Incredible, amazing…safe." The layers of fears she had carried for so long began to drop off one by one, until only peace and contentment remained. They didn't have to say a word. Their hearts had already spoken. She and Bryson sat in comfortable silence, the swing gently moving back and forth, until her mother called them in to eat.

"I have some sweet tea, Bryson. Is that okay?" her mother asked.

Raven laughed at the look on Bryson's face. Clearly he hadn't believed what she had told him about her mother.

"Sweet tea is just fine, Mrs. Holloway. You shouldn't have gone through all this trouble."

Raven met his stunned gaze with an amused one. "Mom, you really went overboard." She had made fried chicken, potato salad, fresh green beans and homemade biscuits. She'd mentioned making the biscuits for dinner.

Her mother waved her off. "Oh, this isn't much."

Bryson's smile widened and Raven rolled her eyes.

"Is there a place where I can wash up?" Bryson asked.

"Of course, baby."

*Baby?* Her mother was going too far.

Her mother pointed Bryson in the direction of the half bath down the hall. As soon as he was out of hearing range, she turned to Raven. "Oh, my goodness! He's grown up to be such a handsome young man." She giggled like a schoolgirl. "And when did you start dating? You always told me the two of you were only good friends."

"It happened about a month ago. Took us both by surprise."

She clasped her hands together. "Lord, I'm going to have some pretty grandbabies."

Raven's eyes widened. "*Mom,*" she whispered, taking a hasty glance into the hallway to make sure Bryson hadn't heard. She sighed. "Can you please keep it down?"

"What? Bryson is a cutie."

She threw up her hands. No way would she win this battle. Bryson re-entered the kitchen and she hoped he missed her mother's last statement.

"You should probably go and wash your hands, Raven. Oh, and your dad will be here in time for lunch. He's anxious to see

Bryson. Isn't that wonderful?"

"Just peachy."

Bryson laughed softly.

Afraid of what else her outrageous mother might say if left alone with Bryson, Raven walked over to the kitchen sink to wash her hands. They had just sat down at the dining room table when she heard her father open the screen door.

He poked his head in the dining room and waved. "Let me wash up and I'll be right there." Her father was back in a minute.

Bryson quickly came to his feet.

"Dad, you remember Bryson Montgomery. Bryse, my dad, Allen Holloway."

"It's a pleasure to see you again, sir," Bryson said and extended his hand.

Her father grasped the proffered hand and smiled, evidently pleased by Bryson's manners. "Same here, son. It's been a few years. Looking forward to talking to you later."

Meeting his gaze easily, Bryson said, "As am I, sir."

Raven wanted to sink into the floorboards. They were acting like she was sixteen and going on her first date. Bryson reached under the table and gave her hand a gentle squeeze, letting her know it was okay. His touch sent calming vibes through her and she relaxed.

* * *

Bryson woke up Saturday morning with a huge smile on his face. He liked Raven's parents and had enjoyed spending time with them. He thought about the conversation he'd had with Mr. Holloway. The man had grilled him for nearly an hour, but Bryson hadn't minded because he had no doubts he would pass every test. In an age when asking for a woman's hand didn't occur as much, it had impressed her father that Bryson had chosen to do so.

He checked his pants pocket again to make sure he had everything then called the contact at Rosewood Estates Simeon had given him. Simeon had proven to be a great coconspirator for what he had planned and every person Simeon suggested had been eager to help. His cell rang.

"What's up, baby?" he asked when he answered.

"I'm here," Raven said.

"Okay. I'll be right down." Bryson's heart started beating rapidly. He took a deep breath and left to go meet his future wife. His steps slowed when he saw her in the lobby. Raven had on golden colored sundress and flat sandals. As he came closer, he saw that the color seemed to bring out the gold highlights in her hair, which hung straight around her shoulders. He smiled and placed a soft kiss on her lips.

Raven smiled sultrily. "I thought I'd let you see a little leg."

"And later, I'm going to show you just how much I appreciate it." They walked hand-in-hand out the front and set off for Rosewood Estates. The inn was located in the heart of downtown only a block from the estate. Once at the estate, he led Raven in the opposite direction of the garden.

"I thought we were going to walk in the garden," Raven said.

"We can do that, too. But you mentioned the lake being your favorite spot, so I thought we could start there."

"Okay." Excitement sparkled in her eyes. "How did the conversation go with my dad last night?"

"Fine. Just like I said it would. He wanted to be sure I had your best interest at heart and since I always have, I didn't have any problems answering his questions."

"My parents like you, especially my mom, in case you couldn't tell."

"I like them, too. And you already know how my parents feel about you." His parents lived in LA and she had been to their house several times.

"Have you…?" her voice trailed off.

He stopped. "We were interrupted before, so I decided to recreate what was supposed to be a special evening." He had everything—rose petals, champagne in an ice bucket, two glasses on coasters and milk and white chocolate covered strawberries—except the fireplace. But the warm weather would suffice. "Have a seat."

Raven sat, removed her shoes and tucked her legs beneath her.

Bryson followed suit. He poured the champagne and fed her a strawberry. "I know how much you like your strawberries with the two kinds of chocolates."

"Mmm, I do." She sipped the champagne. Setting her glass on a coaster, she picked up a strawberry and offered it to him.

When he bit it, some of the juice dripped down onto his bottom lip. She snaked her tongue out and licked it off. With lightning speed, he charged into her mouth, seeking her tongue and sucking gently on it. They both moaned. He was about two seconds from spreading her out on the blanket, so he broke off the kiss. "Unless you want to give the entire town something to talk about, we need to slow down."

"I don't care," Raven said breathlessly.

Bryson smiled. "Behave." Unable to resist, he kissed her again, tenderly, softly. Easing back, he took her hand. "From the first day we met, I knew you were special. At the time, I didn't realize just how much you would impact my life. You've been my sounding board, my confidante, my best friend and now the woman who has completely captured my heart. I want to spend the rest of my life loving you, protecting you and being your safe haven. Marry me, Raven. Embrace forever with me." He withdrew the small ring box from his pocket and opened it.

"Bryse," she whispered then nodded. "Yes, I'll embrace forever with you."

He slid the ring on her finger. "I have one more thing for you." He handed her another small box.

She opened it and gasped. "A lock for the fence. And you had it engraved with our names." She knocked him backwards on the blanket, kissing him with a passion that stole his breath. He'd found that one. And she'd been there the whole time.

# *Epilogue*

*Three weeks later*

"You may now kiss your bride."

Not caring about the audience, Raven threw her arms around Bryson and locked her mouth on his. She vaguely heard her brother clear his throat, but she kept right on kissing him.

When they finally came up for air, Mac said, "Now that's what I'm talking about!"

Bryson looked down at Raven. "You keep that up and we *will* be skipping the reception. As it is, I'm going to have a hard time keeping my hands off you in that dress."

She smiled. The sleeveless dress had a lace bodice front, but the wide keyhole opening left the upper portion of her back bare. And because she knew how much he liked seeing "some leg," the thigh-high slit had given him plenty of it when she walked up the aisle. Unbeknownst to her, he had gotten together with the staff at the estate and delivered the lakefront wedding at sunset she had fantasized about all her life. After the minister's presentation, she hooked her arm in his and walked back up the aisle.

They received hugs from their parents and other family members. She teased Jerome about being the last man standing in their circle, as Kendrick had recently gotten engaged.

Raven excused herself from Bryson for a moment to talk to her girlfriends. She stopped first to thank Ava. "I don't know what to say. I couldn't ask for a better friend."

"Same here," Ava said, hugging her. "Be happy, Raven."

"I am." Someone called out to Ava and she was off. Raven chuckled and continued toward Mac, Quinn and Ryleigh.

"Group hug," Quinn said when she approached.

These women had been part of her life since forever and she didn't know how she would have made it without their friendship. "Thank you so much for being here with me."

"Oh, girl, you know we wouldn't have been anywhere else," Ryleigh said. She had interrupted her business trip to fly in just for the wedding and had to leave early in the morning to get back.

Mac sidled up next to Raven. "I left you a little box at the front desk at the inn. I'm sure Bryson will enjoy it."

Raven glanced over her shoulder and found Bryson staring at her. The look in his eyes made the space between her thighs throb.

"Mmm hmm, he's *really* going to enjoy it."

"Mac, I don't know what I'm going to do with you." They all laughed, but Raven noticed the hint of sadness in Quinn's eyes. She grasped Quinn's hand and gave it a reassuring squeeze. Her time was coming, and soon.

Raven made her way back to where Bryson stood talking with Jerome and Kendrick. He saw her and met her halfway.

"Hello, Mrs. Montgomery."

When he kissed her, all the love she felt for him overflowed in her heart. She thought herself the luckiest woman in the world. She'd married her best friend. And he was hers. Forever.

# Dear Reader

I hope you are enjoying the Once Upon A Bridesmaid series. They say best friends make the best lovers and that's certainly true in my case, even though I never saw it coming…lol. Maybe I'll share that story with you someday in person. Raven and Bryson find themselves in a similar situation and it's going to be an interesting ride to see if they can bridge the friendship-to-lover gap. If they're lucky, forever just may be in the cards.

I had such a blast collaborating with Sherelle, Angie and Elle and can't wait to do it again. Be sure to let us know what you think.

Thank you for your continued encouragement and support. I appreciate you. Remember to drop me a line at sheryllister@gmail.com if you have any questions, comment, or just want to chat. I love hearing from you.

You can also find me:

Website: www.sheryllister.com
Facebook: www.facebook.com/sheryllisterauthor
Twitter: @1slynne
Instagram: sheryllister

Love & Blessings!

Sheryl

## Discover More by Sheryl Lister

**Once Upon A Bridesmaid Series**

*Yours Forever (Book 1) by Sherelle Green*
*Beyond Forever (Book 2) by Elle Wright*
*Embracing Forever (Book 3) by Sheryl Lister*
*Hopelessly Forever (Book 4) by Angela Seals*

Harlequin Kimani

*Just To Be With You*
*All Of Me*
*It's Only You*
*Be Mine For Christmas (Unwrapping The Holidays Anthology)*
*Tender Kisses (The Grays of Los Angeles Book 1)*
*Places In My Heart (The Grays of Los Angeles Book 2)*
*Giving My All To You (The Grays of Los Angeles Book 3)*

Other Titles

*Made To Love You*
*It's You That I Need*
*Perfect Chemistry*

## About the Author

Sheryl Lister is a multi-award winning author who has enjoyed reading and writing for as long as she can remember. After putting writing on the back burner for several years, she became serious about her craft in 2009. When she's not reading or writing, Sheryl can be found on a date with her husband or in the kitchen creating appetizers and bite-sized desserts. Sheryl resides in California and is a wife, mother of three and former pediatric occupational therapist. She is a member of RWA, CIMRWA, the Kiss of Death Chapter of RWA, and is represented by Sarah E. Younger of Nancy Yost Literary Agency.

CPSIA information can be obtained
at www.ICGtesting.com
Printed in the USA
LVHW02s1544200418
574265LV00009B/422/P